GABRIEL'S WELL

GABRIEL'S WELL

BLAINE M. YORGASON

Shadow Mountain
Salt Lake City, Utah

Library of Congress Cataloging-in-Publication Data

Yorgason, Blaine M., 1942-
    Gabriel's well / Blaine M. Yorgason.
        p. cm.
ISBN 1-57345-641-1

1. Frontier and pioneer life--West (U.S.)--Fiction. 2. Fathers and sons--
Fiction. I. Title.

PS3575.O57 G33 2000
813'.54--dc21

                                                                99-088644

Printed in the United States of America   18961-6637

10   9   8   7   6   5   4   3   2   1

FICTION   119828

For Judy O—
my sister and my friend

Acknowledgments

Though I take full responsibility for the following account, I express deep appreciation for the support and insights of Ronald Millett, Sheri Dew, and Timothy Robinson, as well as all the others at Shadow Mountain who have made my dream their own.

For historical background and information, I am grateful, first, to the writer George Kennan, whose article "Have Reservation Indians Any Vested Rights?" was originally published in *Outlook* on 29 March 1902. The full text can be found in *The Annals of America, Volume 12, 1895–1904* (Chicago: Encyclopaedia Britannica, Inc., 1968), pp. 476–82.

Second, Ida M. Tarbell, whose writings exposed the social and business evils and injustice at the turn of the last century, was also of great help. The full text of the Tarbell article I used for this piece was taken from *The History of the Standard Oil*

Company (New York, 1904, Volume 2, pp. 256–92), and is also reprinted in the same volume of *Annals* quoted above (pp. 535–41).

Third, the sunflower and tomato stories that follow, while horribly pulverized, are actually part of Great Plains folklore, and were collected in various forms and versions in the 1930s under the W.P.A. by the Federal Writers' Project. More recently they have been reprinted in Roger Welsch, *Shingling the Fog and Other Plains Lies* (Lincoln: University of Nebraska Press, 1972), pp. 62–63.

Finally, I express appreciation to editors LeRoy R. Hafen and Glen Rounds for their comprehensive treatment of mountain man biographies, language, tall tales, and way of life during the 18th and 19th centuries. Their books, respectively, are titled: *The Mountain Men and the Fur Trade of the Far West,* 10 vols. (Glendale, Ca.: The Arthur H. Clark Company, 1972); and *Mountain Men: George Frederick Ruxton's Accounts of Fur Trappers and Indians in the Rockies* (New York: Holiday House, 1966).

PART ONE

1

There! Somebody was standing by the old cottonwood tree at the back of our yard! The brilliant flash of lightning had revealed him clearly—bib overalls tight to his skin, a slouched hat across his eyes. As the lightning and thunder crashed around me a moment later, I realized I had glimpsed somebody else, too, crouched twenty feet above on the big limb where Father had tied our swing—

The rain was falling in torrents, just as it had earlier when it had washed out our baseball game. Though the wind was whipping cold rain onto me through the screens that surrounded our back porch, I felt rooted to the floorboards, unable to move.

Minutes earlier a pounding had brought me straight up out of a dreamless sleep, and in an instant I had known it was the wind banging the porch door, which I had forgotten to latch. With a groan I had pulled the covers over my head, but the drumming of rain on the roof and the moaning of wind under our eaves had not let me return to sleep. Then the loose door was pounding again, and I had staggered to my feet and made my way past my parents' bedroom, down the stairs, through the kitchen, and out onto the back porch.

Fighting the shock of the cold rain, I had just reached for the latch when the sudden sight of two specters by the tree—not a hundred feet from me—had frozen me where I stood, barely breathing, waiting for the next flash of lightning before I ran for help.

The lightning flashed again and our backyard was lit brilliant as noonday. Quickly my eyes scanned the illuminated yard. But there was no one there—not by the tree, not on the swing limb, not beside the gate—not anywhere! Even more strange, I had seen in that same flash of light that the porch door had been latched tightly, and could not have been banging at all.

Ducking back inside the kitchen, I threw the bolt on the door to the porch and was just heading for the stairs when the pounding came again—from directly in front of me this time!

Again I froze, and then I heard Father's feet hit the floor above me.

"Ezekiel," I heard my mother question anxiously, "who on earth could it be?"

Father's answer was low enough that I couldn't hear the words. Then his footsteps creaked along the dark hall and descended the stairs. Not seeing me pressed against the wall, he lit the hallway lamp, knocked back the latch, and pulled open the front door.

There on the veranda was a soaked and bedraggled man wearing a dark overcoat, his collar pulled up against the rain. But he was alone, and he wore neither a hat nor denim overalls, which meant either that somebody else was still out there in the dark and the rain or that my overactive imagination had once again gotten the best of me.

"Pardon me, sir," he said, "but I fear that I am more mud-splattered than otherwise, and must be a fright to see. For that I am sorry. I also apologize for the lateness of the hour, but I was told that you are the Town Recorder?"

From behind Father I could see little but hear everything, and though the visitor's English was perfect, there was a trace of something in it that sounded studied and foreign.

"Among other things," Father replied as he drew his housecoat more tightly about himself.

"Well, sir," the man continued, "then you and I must do some urgent business regarding a certain parcel of land. I repeat, sir, this is terribly important—"

"It isn't so important that it cannot wait for you to come indoors," Mother interrupted as she swept down the dimly lit stairs. "Cluvarous, stop cowering against that wall and go build up the fire in the kitchen." Father turned around then and for the first time realized that I had been behind him.

"Ezekiel, dear," Mother continued, "would you please fetch some dry clothing for this gentleman— something warm? He looks to be about your size. And you, sir. Please remove your boots and wrap there at the door. Once you are changed you may come into the kitchen. I will soon have something prepared to warm you."

Without waiting for an answer, Mother bustled past me to the kitchen, and as I hurried to follow I saw the raised eyebrow Father was giving her. She merely smiled and glanced back to wink one of her dusky, almost black eyes at him. Slowly and deliberately he closed the door behind the stranger, helped him out of his coat and boots, and then moved off to gather together some warm clothing.

Angry over the fact that Mother had practically called me a coward, I nevertheless lit the coal-oil lamp and stirred up the still-hot coals in the cooking stove. With the front stove lid off, I dumped in chips and kindling, blew up a few flames, and then backed out of Mother's way. Wandering over to the kitchen window, I squinted out into the darkness, trying to see past the porch to the old cottonwood tree. But all I could make out was darkness and the pounding rain.

"Mr. and Mrs. Jones," the stranger said as he followed Father into the kitchen a few moments later, "this really isn't necessary, you know. All along I have been planning on staying at the boardinghouse in town."

"Oh, stuff and nonsense!" Mother declared in her best schoolmarm voice, which though friendly left no doubt whatsoever that she was in charge. "We have a main-floor bedroom that sits empty year in and year out, and there is no reason that you shouldn't use it. Now, you have the advantage of us, sir, in that you know our names."

The young man smiled broadly, and I remember thinking that I had never seen such clear blue eyes, straight white teeth, or jet-black hair, now wild and curly against the fair skin of his forehead. He was an amazingly handsome man.

"You are right, Mrs. Jones, and I do apologize. My name is Jose Maria Carlos Louis Rivera Sebastian de Ortega Rejos, Americanized as Carlos de Ortega. You may call me Carlos."

I was stunned! I had never heard such a name in my life. What an embarrassment! My own name, Cluvarous, was bad enough, but I could never have endured a name such as his. So I stared at him shamelessly, wondering how he had managed to grow all the way to adulthood with it, while Mother sat him at our table. And I was still staring when Father sat down across from him and accepted his own steaming cup of the terribly expensive European hot chocolate that Mother had recently ordered from a mail-order catalogue. Of course I didn't expect to receive my own cup. That treat was reserved for Sunday evenings.

"That's quite a name you have," Father said softly as he cradled his cup in his hands. His manner was reserved, which was unusual for Father, and I remember wondering what was troubling him.

Again the young man smiled. "Spanish. Castillian,

in fact. Or at least it started out that way a few generations ago. Most wonder that my first two names are Joseph and Mary, and so by habit I explain it. The tired old priest who baptized me thought it a good omen to attach the names of the Holy Family to every male infant he ever baptized. Naturally I never use them, but they are an integral part of my name."

Father nodded his understanding. "Well, Carlos, some of us do about the same in these parts, though not as officially. My given name is Ezekiel, but folks just call me Zeke, and you are welcome to do the same. Young Cluvarous here prefers Clue, thinking Cluvarous pompous and stuffy, and my lovely wife Abigail insists on being called just that—Abigail. Our daughter JudyAnn is upstairs asleep—miraculously, I might add, because of this storm—and she is JudyAnn to everyone but Clue, who calls her Jude. Sometimes, though, I call her Sis. She's just nine, you see, and Cluvarous here is eleven." Turning, he smiled at me and ruffled my already wild hair. "Say 'How do you do,' Cluvarous."

I nodded instead.

Father took a short sip from his cup, smacking his lips at the piping hot liquid. "My office is not here in my home, Carlos, and since this is Friday, and Monday is the Fourth of July, I won't be in my office until Tuesday morning. But if you would like, I'd be happy to at least learn the nature of your urgent business. Should it warrant it, I'm certain a little Saturday work might be in order."

The young man nodded anxiously. "Mr. Jones—Zeke," he began, searching for his words, "I'm a geologist, a scientist who studies rocks. I took my degree at Stanford University, and I now work for a large eastern oil company. They have me doing exploratory work, traveling around the country in an effort to discover new and untapped fields of petroleum, which they then exploit with wells."

At this point Mother placed a heaping platter of cookies on the table between the two men, which quite naturally caught my eleven-year-old attention. In the last year or so Mother had instituted in our home at least a hundred rules regarding proper decorum for young gentlemen and ladies, and one of the most cardinal was that we did not take food, especially sweets, that had been set out for guests. But, oh, did those cookies look good!

"Of course you know how important petroleum is becoming to the growth and industry of our entire country," Carlos continued. "By the end of this year—1904—our nation's petroleum consumption will have doubled since the turn of the century. Because of that, you can see that my work is terribly important."

Father nodded but remained silent, waiting.

"My reason for dragging you folks out of bed at such a terrible hour is that I believe I have discovered in this area a major petroleum field, a veritable ocean of oil. If I am right, this field will generate vast amounts of petroleum to fuel our nation's industries, our transportation systems, and even our homes. For you fine, progressive-minded people in this area, it will mean undreamed-of wealth and prosperity. Your little town will become an important city on anyone's map, the railroad will beat a path to your door, and soon you will have all the amenities of advanced civilization right here around you—doctors, hospitals, universities, industry, gas street lamps, and in every home you will have electrical lighting, oil furnaces, and even telephones. There will be no need to go elsewhere for any of these things. You can see, now, why I feel such an urgency about this."

"And you are certain that this nearby oil field you have discovered will produce petroleum?"

"I believe I can declare it without hesitation!"

Father nodded. "Interesting. No one I know of

has ever seen much sign of oil—at least not around here."

"They haven't known what to look for," Carlos declared, after which he launched into a long and intellectual explanation of how hydrocarbons— crude petroleum and natural gas—are formed. I heard little of it, however, for by then I had noticed Carlos's hands, which seemed to be as important to his way of speaking as his mouth. In all my life I have never seen anyone use his hands so fluidly to punctuate and elaborate on what he was saying. It was almost as if Carlos's hands were directing his words and not the other way around. "Am I making this clear enough?" he asked suddenly.

Father smiled but said nothing. Mother was silent too. She was probably understanding Carlos, and I was trying to—sort of. But those expressive hands of his, not to mention the huge platter of cookies that sat mostly untouched beneath them, made it hard for me to concentrate.

Carlos went on, describing things such as source rocks, oil's natural upward migration to reservoir rocks, the La Brea Tar Pits near Los Angeles in California, where oil had seeped through to the surface, and underground caprocks, which prevented such seepage in most other areas. Both my folks made occasional comments, but I didn't speak a word, not wanting to appear foolish. Besides, Carlos was using words I had never even heard of, and I didn't want him to know it. Apparently my expression betrayed my ignorance, however, for after looking at me he turned and asked Mother if he might have a pencil and a sheet of paper.

"There are various sorts of traps where reservoir rock exists," he continued as he began drawing a series of mostly parallel lines across the page with a little pine tree growing out of the top one, thus indicating the surface of the earth. He then explained what he called stratigraphic traps. "These small ellipses or circles that I am drawing, Clue, represent such traps: holes or empty spaces in the stone where hydrocarbons have migrated or gathered up to, and then have been stopped by the harder caprock above them. It is into these hydrocarbon-filled traps or holes that my company sinks its wells."

Amazed that he was making an explanation expressly for me, I crowded closer to the table—and unfortunately the cookies.

Carlos suddenly reached for one, lifted it, and gave me a sly wink. Then to my amazement he handed it to me—completely circumventing

Mother's rules of decorum and earning my enduring devotion.

"One such trap," he went on as he drew a second diagram under a squiggly tree, "occurs near what is called a salt dome. Rock salt is a low-density sedimentary rock, and when deeply buried beneath more dense sediments such as sand and mud, it rises toward the surface of the earth in vast pillars or bulges known as salt domes. As the rock salt rises, it penetrates and deforms the overlying rock layers, causing a bulge in the earth's surface and forming structures or cavities along its underground margins that trap petroleum and gas."

"And today you found our Dome," Father stated quietly while I chewed the last of the cookie.

"Our Dome?" I blurted in surprise, swallowing hard to empty my mouth before speaking again. "That useless country out south of town's a salt dome?"

"Yes, Clue," Father replied quietly, as if he knew every bit as much as the geologist.

I had occasionally wondered about the strange, almost treeless dome, but had never supposed there might be salt out there. It was a barren lift-up of hilly country that began ten or twelve miles south of town, a bone-dry land that didn't support much but a bit of brush, a coyote or two, and a few long-eared rabbits that gave the coyotes something to chase.

"Actually, Zeke," Carlos said, smiling widely, "I discovered your dome several days ago, and have been tramping about on it ever since, making certain. The barren land is an indicator of salt, and what little water I found is brackish, while your stream here in the valley is fresh. I have no doubt that I have found a massive salt dome—a veritable guarantee of an ocean of oil hidden below."

Abruptly the man's smile vanished. "Now, here is the important part, at least for you folks. If the land on and around that dome is already legally owned, then the owners are going to be fabulously wealthy. If it is part of the public domain, then I intend to file claim to it in behalf of my company." Suddenly his eyes twinkled in a way that let us know we were hearing something that was for us to hear, and no one else. "That is, I will file unless the good folks of your community happen to record a legal claim before I can get to it next Tuesday."

Father's eyes grew wide, and he leaned back in his chair. "Why this great act of generosity?" he asked.

Carlos's hands lifted with his smile, and the

combination of the two caused his whole being to glow with kindness. "Frankly, my company is wealthy, and this discovery will make them even more so. On the other hand, this is a small, out-of-the-way community of good people, most of whom struggle to make ends meet. Because I grew up poor, I understand the difficulties of it and take every opportunity to see that others are as blessed as the oil company and I have been.

"Zeke," he then declared, sounding as if he had known Father for years and years, "it was customary among my Castillian ancestors to reward—quite handsomely—I might add, those who showed them kindness. Insofar as it is legal and within my power, I maintain that custom. You and Abigail and young Cluvarous have been extremely kind to me this night. I am asking quite humbly that you accept my gratitude."

Slowly Father exhaled his breath. "Are you suggesting," he finally questioned, "that I take personal advantage of this information you have given us?" His voice was quiet and severe.

Carlos paused. His smile suddenly disappeared, and his hands fluttered close to his chest. "Of a truth, and I hope you will forgive my bold speech, I would far rather see the royalties paid only to the two of you, instead of diluting them among so many as an entire town."

The room grew quiet. For some reason I glanced at Mother, and I was surprised to see that her chest was heaving as if she had run a long race. Her eyes seemed unusually bright as she gazed at Carlos.

Father, on the other hand, was still as death, except that he was softly drumming the fingers of his right hand on the table. But his face was without expression, and he wasn't looking at anything but the table beneath where his fingers were beating their quiet tattoo.

It was Father who finally broke the silence. "Mr. de Ortega," he said with soft formality as he reached for a cookie, which he bit into and began to chew. "These are interesting things to consider."

"Yes," Carlos agreed, taking two cookies and again handing one of them to me, "and it is certainly convenient that you have three entire days in which to consider them."

For a moment Father and Mother looked at each other, and something passed between them. "Not that those three days will be needed," Father responded as Mother's breath stopped and her hand went involuntarily to her temple. "You see, sir, that land has already been filed on, deeded and recorded—by a couple of people we here in town call the Hurryups."

"Ah, yes, the Indians!" Carlos's smile had not diminished even a little, and yet somehow it had changed. His eyes had narrowed, his lips had thinned, and for a second or so he seemed like an entirely different man. But then I must have blinked, for when I looked again he appeared exactly as he had before—youthful, concerned, sincere.

"I ran into those people a few times during my exploration. Very strange; very strange, indeed." Carefully Carlos pulled a sheet of paper from a thin leather folio he had brought to the table. "May I read you a little something that I just happen to have with me?"

"Of course."

"This is a quote from Senator Rawlins, who, as you may know, assists in directing the affairs of the Indian Office of the Interior Department. It was published in *Outlook,* and is dated March 29, 1902." Again Carlos beamed his radiant smile.

"Senator Rawlins, who is speaking of a Federal law that was passed a year or so ago, says, and I quote:

Indians . . . are wards of the government. This bill . . . converts their land into a fund which applies to their benefit [because] they cannot intelligently deal with [it] independently . . . The Court of Appeals of the District of Columbia held last week that "the treaty of 1868" . . . certainly did not vest in the Indians, either in their individual or tribal capacity, anything more than the right to occupy the land . . . There was no grant of estates, either freehold or leasehold—only a mere right to occupy and use the lands.

"It seems obvious," Carlos went on as he lowered the paper and slid it back into his folio, "that the law Senator Rawlins speaks of completely eliminates our dilemma."

"May I see that paper?" Father quietly asked.

"See it?" Carlos was taken back by Father's request. But, seeing no way out, he slowly retrieved the document and handed it to Father.

"Interesting, Mr. de Ortega. You—or someone, at least—seems to have had quite a time manipulating the words of this quote. Quite naturally I am reluctant to accept it at face value."

"Are you questioning my integrity?"

"No. But I am concerned about this alleged quote."

"I assure you, sir, that it accurately reflects Senator Rawlins's message, and you are welcome to go to the original source for verification. To the best of my understanding, it is totally illegal for Indians to hold title to any property anywhere, either by ownership or lease. More, because your state has no reservations, Indians have no right even to occupy land around here! Am I not correct?"

Father nodded slowly. "Yes, sir, despite the injustice of it, I believe that is correct."

"Then," and now Carlos's smile grew confident again, "I don't see the problem."

"It isn't much of one." Father's voice was still and quiet. "Not unless you want ownership of that land to change."

"Excuse me?"

Father smiled warmly. "The fact of the matter is, sir, that the Hurryups aren't Indians. Never have been, never will be."

The geologist's smile thinned once again. "You seem awfully certain, Zeke. How is it that you became privy to this important information?"

"They told me."

For the first time that night Carlos laughed—a delightful laugh that made me think of ringing bells. "Zeke, it's wonderful that you trust people so thoroughly. Of course it ought to make the owner of your bank a little nervous—" Carlos chuckled again. "But still, I assume that you have a fine, sound judgment in most things, for your bank is certainly prospering."

"The bank is doing all right," Father declared distantly.

"Of course it is. Besides, I couldn't help but notice that fine new Packard automobile you have under canvas cover outside, so you yourself must be doing quite well." He smiled innocently. "As I understand it, there is only one other automobile in town. That is quite an accomplishment, Zeke. Very admirable! I would imagine that folks hereabouts respect you because of it. More, I would suppose you are as generous with others as you are with yourself."

Father merely looked at him.

"And now," Carlos continued without hesitation, "you have been presented with an opportunity to make a *real* contribution to this wonderful little town. You have the opportunity of helping them by spreading your own wealth even farther—in fact, as far as you may wish to spread it. No longer will the owners of your bank, the Pursemans, be the only ones here who are known for their wealth. Instead it will be the Jones family, followed distantly by the Pursemans! You will be known far and wide, both of you, and through your largesse you will be a blessing to everyone in town and elsewhere."

"I have already explained—"

Carlos waved his expressive hands, stopping Father in mid-sentence. "I know you are troubled by this, Zeke. I can see it in your eyes. But I tell you, it is not only possible for you to assume this wealth, it is imperative! You see, I have also done some research—quite a bit, in fact. And I swear to you that despite whatever those Hurryup people may have told you, they are, in fact as well as fancy, Indians! And frankly, Zeke—and I am sure you will understand the ramifications of this—it is not only illegal for them to own land, but it is just as illegal for someone such as yourself to attempt to record property illegally deeded to them!"

Father shook his head stubbornly, and I noticed that Mother's breathing was growing more deep than ever, a sure sign that she was upset. "I am sorry, Mr. de Ortega," Father affirmed, "but I believe you are wrong."

"I am never wrong, not about this sort of thing!" Carlos's smile had finally vanished, and his eyes seemed to flash with intensity. "Those people hold no legal right to property, and you had better believe it. If you choose to oppose me in this, then I promise you, Zeke, I shall immediately begin to discuss certain matters with the other citizens of your community, matters that will include your surprisingly prosperous circumstances and your questionable involvement with those two Indians. And I assure you, sir, they *will* believe!"

At Carlos's dire announcement, Mother made a small sound back in her throat, almost like a moan or a whimper. And then, to my everlasting surprise, she collapsed in a heap on the kitchen floor.

2

Carlos stood, and Father rushed to gather Mother into his arms. I fetched a glass of water, which Father trickled down her throat, and in a few moments she revived. But seeing her sprawled out on our floor filled me with a terrible sense of foreboding.

I had always thought of her as a wonderful mother, but for some reason she and I had been having difficulties of late—difficulties that I couldn't understand. Of course she was terribly busy, with sick headaches growing more frequent, and I know Father thought pressure or stress was the problem. Not alone was she the schoolmarm through the winter, but year round she was an active member of the "Books, Bridge and Thimble Society" as well as the "Daughters of Our Pioneers," "Chautauqua," and "Industrial Progress for Our

Community" clubs. She was on our town fair committee as well as the committee for the better education of wayward children. And that year she was president of the "Fourth of July American Independence Day Celebration and Parade Committee," which she was about to turn into the grandest celebration our town had ever seen.

Besides that, she was one of the prettiest ladies in town, an opinion shared by more than one or two of the other fellows near my age. In fact, until recently I had thought she was tons prettier, even, than the Gibson girls, those famous caricatures of women drawn and published in newspapers and magazines by the artist Charlie Gibson. And Mother was real, whereas Gibson's girls were only drawings modeled after Alice Roosevelt, Teddy's impetuous, free-spirited daughter.

Of course Mother had remade herself to look like the Gibson girl illustrations, too, and to be honest, that bothered me. Olive complexioned, she kept her dark hair pompadoured atop her head, and her head was always poised above a throat that, as Father used to put it, even Aphrodite would envy. Like the drawings, Mother was tall and stately, always superbly dressed, and, also according to

Father, she was artful in social gatherings without ever being truly wicked.

But whenever I saw her in public, putting on airs, as I called it, I couldn't help but think about her other side—the side that no one but me was ever allowed to see. No matter what I did, I seemed to be in trouble with her, and no matter how I tried to explain myself, it only made things worse.

"Cluvarous Jones!" she frequently seethed, holding her left hand up to her temple the way she did when one of her sick headaches was coming on, "Mind your manners!" or "Use proper English!" or "Stop persecuting your little sister!"

Or when I complained about my awful name: "Why, Cluvarous Ezekiel Jones, I declare! Cluvarous is a perfectly good name—stately, in fact, not at all like the awful names of some of the rougher element in this town. I found it in a fine old book of Latin verse, and it will do nothing but add dignity to you all the days of your life!"

Dignity, I thought with scorn. Who the double-edged deuce cared about dignity? All I wanted was to be like everyone else—to have a few friends and to be accepted by them as an equal. That was why I had been pleading for a year or more to have my own dog. Every other boy in town had a dog who followed him around all day long, while all I had was my dumb little sister. And with her tagging along, I couldn't even ride my bicycle—which was nearly as bad as not having my own mutt. But Mother wouldn't hear of it, calling all dogs flea-carrying mongrels and my little sister's presence essential to my leaving the house for any reason whatsoever.

"Mother," I would then plead, doing my best to sound proper and educated the way she liked, "just as you prefer Mother over Mom and Father prefers Pop over Father and Zeke over Ezekiel, I prefer Clue over Cluvarous. See? Clue, like they find in that new Sir Arthur Conan Doyle mystery book you ordered in for me to read last winter."

"Young man," she would then breathe venomously while I cringed before her, "you are still a child, and children are impressionable. I don't want you to ever forget that you are a Jones, and that I intend for you to grow up to be a gentleman like your father." That was a word she used often in these talks, and sometimes I wondered if there was anything worse than not being a gentleman.

"If I allowed you to vulgarize your name, you would become exactly like the rougher element in this town—unproductive, despised, pitied, ignored—

growing more crude and coarse all the time! Therefore, you will do well to remember that I am Mother to you, and your father is J. Ezekiel Jones, Esquire! Vulgar nicknames for your parents will never do! Nor will they do for you." Again Mother would rub her head. "Why, you are neither Arthur Conan Doyle nor his protagonist, Sherlock Holmes, and you are most certainly not some essentially useless tidbit of information that might be construed by a fictitious detective to mean more than it should. A clue, for goodness sake! Of all the ridiculous notions—"

Father, on the other hand, never seemed to get upset with me no matter what I did. He was even taller than Mother, trim and dignified-looking, in every way a gentleman. He was also bright, and was constantly endeavoring to develop his mind. In fact, he jokingly called himself an etymologist—a person who studies words—and he was always encouraging JudyAnn and me to do the same. He had spent several years working toward a Doctorate of Philosophy from some eastern university—a Ph.D.—which he never did actually receive. But because we didn't understand what it was, both JudyAnn and I grew up with the impression that Father was studying to be a philosopher.

He and Mother had met in normal school, married upon Father's graduation from college and hers from finishing school, and had happened to pass through our town shortly thereafter while casting about the country looking for a home. They had liked the valley and had almost instantly been offered positions by the town council, Mother as the schoolmarm and Father as clerk in the local bank. Fifteen years had now passed by. Many of Mother's former pupils were already adults, eagerly sending their own children to her classes. And Father had advanced until he was manager of the town's small but financially sound banking institution and also the elected Town Recorder. Until that fateful night, both of my parents had held respected positions in the town and were known throughout the county as important people.

Carlos had spoken of the Hurryups, the Indian tenants who lived out on our dome of salt. Never could we have imagined that our lives would become so entwined with theirs. They were recluses. They lived alone and didn't often come to town. But when they did, their mere presence always caused a stir.

The thing was, by nineteen and ought four, Indians were nonexistent in our part of the country, having been relegated years before to reservations in distant states. The Hurryups, however, had somehow managed to remain behind and escape being rounded up. Of course no one knew for sure what Indian tribe or nation they were supposed to be from, and no one cared. Actually, their features didn't much look Indian at all, but on account of their berry-brown skin, or perhaps because of their having been in the country as long as anyone could remember and still choosing to live out on the Dome, or maybe because of their funny way of talking and dressing, we townfolks always called them Indians.

Truth be known, there was hardly a day went by that I myself didn't make some snickering reference to them. It was a sure way to get a laugh or a smile from those I wanted as my friends; everybody else including grownups did pretty much the same, and so far as I know, none of us ever gave it a second thought. Even Mother did it on occasion, using the Hurryups as a warning of how bad things could become, IF—

As I've said, the Hurryups were reclusive, showing up in town maybe once every three or four months, and then hardly speaking to anyone. And when they did speak, people could hardly understand a word that dropped from their mouths, or so folks liked to say.

I had never actually seen them in person until the day before Carlos had come banging on our door. It happened at the field where we fellows were playing ball—me holding down my usual position in the outfield on account of I was small and not a particularly good player.

In my mind I can see them yet, nodding and smiling and talking sort of funny as they scurried toward me. I'd heard they were always in a hurry, which is where they got their name, and not from any sort of family line. Folks did that in those days, giving each other nicknames on account of some sort of event or distinguishing characteristic from the person's life. For instance, there was our newspaper owner/editor, the perpetually ink-spotted "Spots" Heyermier. Another was Benny Olson, my best childhood friend, who liked to skip rocks across the millpond where his father was the miller. In fact, he was the best rock skipper I ever saw, which earned him the nickname of Skipper, or Skip after he grew up and got married. When he died of old age a few years back, there weren't more than two or three of us left who even knew his real name.

Skipper's father, John Olson, who'd lost his arm in a milling accident long before my time, was known as One-armed John; that was as opposed to Limpy John, who ran the Emporium, and John Scat, a farmer who didn't much like kids and was always telling us to scat when we tried to walk atop his picket fence. There was a host of others, far too numerous to mention.

But the Indians who lived out on that barren lump of salt had come to be known as the Hurryups, and that day when they passed our ball field, they were living up to their name. They were in a gosh-awful hurry, walking faster, almost, than I could run.

At first I didn't even see them. I was too intent on who was up at bat, hoping against hope that I could catch my first-ever fly ball. Then I became aware of a commotion over by the street.

Suddenly both children and adults were fleeing this way and that, one mother swooping down to gather her children up from a game of marbles and whisk them away, urging them forward even as she held her own skirts bunched up so she could run after them. I stood transfixed by the scene, and in that instant the baseball thudded to the earth a dozen feet away and rolled past my feet. Still I did not move, for by then I too could see them, and could see that they were scurrying directly toward me. In fact, I was mesmerized by the very sight of them, and for the moment could think of nothing else—baseball included!

"Howdy-do, laddie," the man squeaked as he strode toward me, at the same time reaching out his thin brown hand to offer a handshake. "'Tis pleased I am to be making your acquaintance!"

Hesitantly I shook his bony hand, surprised that up close he didn't look as young as I had first thought.

"This be me sweet Miss Kizzy," he then squeaked happily as he forcefully directed my hand toward his wife. "Say howdy-do back to her, Cluvarious Jones!"

In amazement I mumbled something that I hoped sounded polite.

"Well, doo-da dah," the frail, dark-skinned woman breathed as she stepped toward me with her own hand thrust forward, using a phrase that I thought should have earned her a most wonderful nickname. "Howdy-do to ye, too, Cluvarious Jones."

"It's Cluvarous," I mumbled as I shook her fingers once, slightly, and then dropped them, "not Clu*various!*"

"Of course it be," the brown-skinned man agreed, still beaming his oblivious delight. "Cluvarious."

With that, both strange individuals cackled, turned, and set forth once again on their rapid striding journey toward town. And me? I just stood there with my mouth hanging open in surprise, not alone because the Indians had known my whole despised name, which in and of itself was astounding enough to leave me speechless, but because I had actually met *them*—the infamous and much-gossiped-about Mr. and Mrs. Hurryup.

Mr. Hurryup was of medium height, nowhere near as tall as Father or Mother, and was very thin and gaunt looking. The skin below his chin hung in folds like the dewlap on an old cow. And that dewlap along with his bony hands were the only parts of the man that made him look old. In every other way he looked to be about the same age as Father, or maybe even younger. He was dressed in bib overalls like most of the working men in town wore, and his red plaid shirt was buttoned tight at his throat and wrists, as if he had been working in the hay and was trying to keep out the dried leaves. Dirty Indian moccasins rather than boots adorned his feet, and they were beaded all fancy, too. His face, berry-brown in color, was whiskerless like an

Indian's face, and he even wore an Indian hat, black and high-crowned with a flat brim, with some sort of long feather tucked into the band.

Except for being shorter and wearing a patched apron over a tight-necked long dress with frayed cuffs at the ends of long sleeves, Mrs. Hurryup looked about like her husband. She was dark-skinned, frail, sort of bony, and had a pinched-looking face that put me in mind of a hungry bird. She too wore beaded moccasins, and her thin, dark hair under her brightly colored scarf was drawn tight in a bun, the way lots of the older women in town wore theirs.

They had no children that anyone had ever seen, but lived in a run-down, ramshackle place out on the Dome. Somehow the Hurryups eked out an existence there, growing a scraggly garden, keeping a few chickens and an old goat, and getting their water from a tiny spring or seep that folks said was pure alkali and tasted just as bitter as dirt. But in spite of that, no matter the weather, no matter the season, nobody ever saw them when they weren't smiling. That was one of the things that made folks nervous, for they were filthy and dirt-poor and had nothing in the world about which to smile.

But there was something else, too, something that stands out in my memory more than any other thing. Impossible as it sounds, the Hurryups never seemed to grow any older! It was said that they had already been living on their hardscrabble range for some time when the first settlers of our little town had stopped their wagons and planted their homes on the creek that ran through our fertile valley. And since a good many of those early folks had already grown old and passed on to their eternal rewards, while the Hurryups were still energetic and youthful looking, one can maybe get an idea of where the notion of their being ageless might have begun. Of course no one knew for sure how old they really were, but it didn't set well with folks, thinking that they might have cast some sort of medicine-man spell or found a fountain of youth or some other such nonsense to stay forever young. All I could say is that from a little distance, as they scurried along in their beaded moccasins making no sound as they went, they looked young as a couple of newlyweds and fresh as daisies on a dewy spring morning. Or at least that is the sarcastic way my mother used to put it.

Others were much less kind.

3

It was much later, and once again the house was still and dark. A very somber Carlos had retired into the spare room downstairs, and now I lay wide awake, listening to the conversation of my parents. But this time I was really listening, for Mother's earlier faint had frightened me, and I was trying to find out what had happened. Unfortunately, that is not what they were discussing.

"Darling, are you certain you are all right?"

"Of course I am all right!" Mother was put out with Father, and the thin wall between our rooms couldn't hide it. "Now stop pestering me about it! Do you hear?"

"Yes, dear."

I could then hear—and thus picture in my mind—Mother repositioning herself on their squeaky bed. "Ezekiel, this decision that you have made is wrong, terribly wrong!"

Father made no answer.

"Ezekiel, do you hear me?"

"I hear you, Abby, but I don't know what you want me to say."

"Of course you do! Carlos is right, and I want you to admit it! Indians are not legally allowed to hold deeds to property—of any kind, anywhere. Whether Carlos's paper has been doctored or not, we know about the court's interpretation of that treaty because we've discussed it. You've even written a letter to Congress concerning your displeasure with it. However, despite what you may personally feel, Ezekiel, that dome cannot legally belong to the Hurryups!"

"I wish I knew why you felt such antagonism toward them."

"It isn't just the Hurryups!" Mother seethed. "I cannot abide people who choose to be dirty and uncouth! Those two Indians are both."

"And so because of that, I should do as Carlos suggests? I should hurry down to the office and file a claim to that ground in my name? Is that what you are saying? You'd feel good about that?"

"J. Ezekiel Jones, why are you talking this way?

Of course I'd feel good about it! Who wouldn't? Besides, Carlos is offering it to us, and you know it."

"He can't offer what he doesn't have. That land belongs to the Hurryups, and has done for years and years and years. Besides which, as I have explained to you at least a dozen times, they are not Indians."

"You don't know that!" Mother's voice was desperate, and I wondered at it. "All you have is their word."

"That's all I have from anyone, Abby, you included."

"Why . . . what on earth do you mean?"

Father took a deep breath, and then slowly exhaled. "I mean I have your word that you will honor our marriage contract," he finally responded, "and you have mine. For fifteen years we have based our lives upon it. If I am to reject the word of the Hurryups simply because the moment seems opportune, would you also have me reject yours the next time you meet a handsome man who seeks to entice you?"

Mother was shocked. "Why, Ezekiel Jones, I declare! That's different, and you know it! We are enlightened people, civilized, progressive! I . . . I can't believe that you would stoop so low as to compare me to a . . . a floozy! I'm telling you, I will not listen to you impugn my honor, my integrity! Because of our spontaneous generosity to Carlos we have a right to that wealth, a perfect right!"

"Abby, it isn't Carlos's wealth to give! That smooth-talking man is trying to steal it."

I could actually hear Mother flouncing on the bed, she was so upset.

"Steal it? Merciful heavens, Ezekiel, that wouldn't be stealing, and you know it! Why, the Hurryups would have no more idea what to do with that kind of wealth, than . . . than fly! They're filthy, uncouth—well, they don't deserve it, they're perfectly happy without it, and most likely they wouldn't want it even if it was offered to them. Besides which, it can't be offered to them in the first place because they're Indians!

"Just remember some of the stories we've heard about the Hurryups through the years. You know as well as I that it has been almost impossible for most Indians to grasp the true value of American goods and services, and living out on the Dome the way they do, those two are no exception. In the Hurryups' hands, the money from that oil would be an utter waste!

"Besides," she continued, her voice pleading, "Carlos was right! Think of all the good we could do with that money! Think of the lives we could bless! Think of the opportunities we could give to Cluvarous and JudyAnn! The best schools, traveling abroad, sound investments that will secure their futures. Or think of the opportunities we could provide for ourselves, for pity's sake! Or the respect we could gain! For once in your life, Ezekiel Jones, stop being so ridiculously generous and think of us!"

For a long moment there was silence, and when Father spoke again, his voice was more quiet, more urgent.

"Abby, Abby, what is happening here? Why have you so suddenly and completely abandoned the simple philosophy that hangs on the wall down in our kitchen—the one you insist on the school-children memorizing each and every year? Remember it, Abby? *'Our business in life is not to see through each other, but to see each other through!'* Think of it, darling, and then think of the things *you* are saying."

"I am," Mother stormed angrily, not persuaded in the least, "and I will not allow a tired old saw like that to dissuade me from the right! Ezekiel, if you love me, you will do whatever it takes to see that the land becomes ours, and not the property of those . . . those *Indians* who have squatted out there!"

The argument seemed to end on that note, and the night grew still, but I remained awake, thinking. I was absolutely convinced that Mother was right, and I couldn't understand why Father was being so stubborn about it. Besides, though I had no clear idea of what being wealthy meant, the thought of an oil furnace and electricity and a real telephone in our home appealed to me. That, and using the money to travel abroad, though the thought of school without Mother as my teacher left me a little cold. Still—

"Ezekiel, are you awake?" Mother suddenly questioned, bringing me wide awake again. "Something's wrong! My head! I . . . I don't—"

Mother's voice faded, the old bed creaked violently, and somehow I knew that Father had crawled to her. "Abby, darling! What is it?"

Without thought I slid to the floor and hurried toward my parents' room. I did not know what had happened to Mother, at least not exactly. But I had every intention of offering whatever help I could give.

"I . . . I'm fine," Mother finally replied, bringing me to an abrupt halt. I was uncertain what to do, so irresolutely I remained against the wall by their open door, eavesdropping without any real intent to do so.

"Are you sure?" Father pressed tenderly.

"Of course I'm sure!" Now Mother was sounding put out again, and I almost smiled my relief. "But I . . . I don't know why you are being so stubborn—"

"I'm being stubborn?" Father chuckled, and then his voice filled with deep concern. "I'm telling you, Abby, this isn't like you. This isn't at all like the woman I married. Why, if you could somehow just listen to yourself! Please, darling, I need you to be the warm, caring, generous woman I have always known. Even more importantly, the children need you to stop being so prejudiced and judgmental. Oh, how they need you! And so do I, darling. I need you to stand beside me in this thing, for I know things that are confidential and cannot be shared, even with you, that would prove I am in the right. Please, please believe me!"

For a long time all I could hear was the silence. Father's big clock was ticking downstairs, and because the rain had stopped I could hear it clearly. But there was no sound coming from my parents' bedroom—no sound at all. Finally Mother spoke again, though her voice was so faint I could hardly hear it.

"Zeke, have . . . have I truly changed, do you think?"

I was as startled by Mother's use of Father's nickname as I was by his reply.

"You have, Abby. I don't know what's brought it about, but it isn't good. The children, Clue especially, are suffering because of it, and I'm worried for all of us."

Again there was silence, and the next thing I heard was the sound of Mother weeping.

"Oh, Ezekiel," she pleaded when she had regained enough control of her voice to speak, "what is happening to me? I know things are changing, but I . . . I don't know what, or why. I feel so confused, and sometimes my head hurts so frightfully I want to scream! And . . . and poor little Clue! I know I am hurting him, but I can't seem to stop myself. He just irritates me all the time, until I think I am going crazy with him! Oh, glory be!

"And now this . . . this Dome dilemma. Is it Carlos, Zeke? Is it him who has pulled me over the edge tonight, or is it myself? I swear I don't know, but for some reason, all that money suddenly seems so much more important to me than those crazy Hurryups. Oh, my darling Ezekiel, whatever is the matter with me?"

The bed creaked again, and in my mind I could see Father holding Mother in his arms, just as he did every time she needed soothing or calming down. "I don't know, sweetheart," he replied, his voice now nearly as quiet as Mother's had become. "One thing, though. I do think you should cut back on your activities—at least for a little while."

"I . . . I feel the same. Right after Monday's parade I will spread the word that other women will need to take over. And I'll tell you something else! Joseph Mary Carlos whatever-else-his-name-is can either give his money to the Hurryups or keep it for himself; I don't care! If you really think I am sounding greedy, then—well, I refuse to allow greed to take over my soul. Why, we already have more than sufficient for our needs—"

And that was about when I sneaked back into my room, crawled under the quilt, and dropped off to sleep for the second time that night. But I did so thinking of the wonderful wealth we had somehow given up to those strange Hurryups—that, and the handsome, dark-haired, blue-eyed Carlos who had come out of the rain and the darkness with such amazing news.

4

"Great catch, Skipper! You got under that one pretty good!"

It was the next morning—Saturday, the second of July, and the day was all that a fellow like me could have asked for. The rain had gone, and it was hot and clear, meadowlarks trilling in the fields all around, farmers' steam engines chugging here and there as they worked their crops, and the air so fresh and clean you could almost taste it.

Skipper Olson, on whom the beauty of the morning seemed to be wasted, nodded without a lot of enthusiasm. "Yeah, I can catch, all right. Now if I could just learn the knack of hitting. Say, Clue, isn't it past time when we're supposed to start?"

Looking up at the sun, I nodded. "Way past. Where do you think everybody is?"

"Beats the stuffing out of me. Hey, JudyAnn, you seen any sign of any of the other fellows?"

My younger sister, who as my only fan had been seated outside the fence but was now scrambling under it and hurrying toward us, shook her head. "No, Skipper. I haven't seen anybody but you two."

Looking puzzled, Skipper walked from home plate toward JudyAnn and me. "It's Saturday, ain't it, Clue? I mean, we didn't get mixed up and come out here on a Sunday, did we?"

"Nope!" I was filled with assurance. "Today's Saturday because last night was Friday night. I know, because that's what Pop told the geologist feller who came late and spent the night in our spare room."

"A geologist? What the heck is that?"

"A scientist who studies rocks," I responded, glad that I had paid at least a modicum of attention.

Skipper's look showed his doubt. "Studies rocks? That sounds nuts—all fruity. Are you making this up, Clue?"

"He isn't making it up," JudyAnn stated defensively. "Mother told me about him this morning when she was looking around for him. She didn't find him, though, because he was already down the road talking to So-Help-Me Hannah."

So-Help-Me Hannah—Hannah Tewksberry, actually—was a single lady who lived down the road from us a quarter of a mile, our closest neighbor. I don't know if she was a widow or a spinster, but she had no children that I'd ever seen, and she was an inveterate gossip, always anxious to spread a juicy story to whomever would listen. And when upset with us youngsters, which seemed often, she had the hilarious habit of placing her hands on her ample hips, wrinkling her nose and beading her eyes down real small, and snarling the phrase, "So help me—" That phrase had become her name, and most folks in town knew her by no other.

"That old busybody?" Skipper snorted at JudyAnn. "What's he talking to So-Help-Me Hannah for?"

"Probably telling her about the petroleum he's discovered out on the Hurryup place," I declared, feeling a little tremor of pride pass through me because I actually knew something few others did. "He says the Dome's caused by salt, and that tons and tons of petroleum are trapped under it, just waiting for wells to pump it out and use it for industry."

"Industry? We don't have any industry around here. We hardly even have a thousand people in the whole town, and that counts farm families and half their livestock. Sounds to me like your geologist friend's as big a storyteller as So-Help-Me Hannah! Oil under the Dome, of all things." Skipper laughed with skepticism, JudyAnn and I joined in, and together the three of us started walking back toward town, determined to find out what had happened to the fellows who had somehow skipped our game.

"Say, there's Baldy," JudyAnn cried as she pointed toward a small group of people standing on the corner.

Our shortstop, Eric "Baldy" Baldwin, was indeed there, along with his folks and his two older sisters—who were both, it was rumored by So-Help-Me Hannah, about to get married, though nobody was certain who the grooms were to be. And the Baldwins were all involved in a deep discussion with Mr. and Mrs. Ernesto Ribaldo and their twin sons, Eeek and Meek, whose real names were Ralph and Norman—our pitcher and catcher, respectively. The Baldwins owned and operated the general store, and Mr. Ribaldo owned the livery stable and a freighting business that had teams and wagons going back and forth between us and the city at least twice a week—usually freighting goods for the general store, my father had once told me.

So it was natural, I thought, that the two families would be visiting with each other.

"Hey, Baldy! Eeek, Meek," I called as I waved and started toward them, "how come you fellers didn't show up at the game today?"

"Shuddup, Clue," Baldy growled while the twins ignored me altogether. "Can't you see we're busy here? Take your dumb sister and get lost!"

Too startled to reply, I backed hurriedly away. "What was that all about?" I asked when I was back beside Skipper and JudyAnn.

"Don't worry about it," Skipper grumbled. "Like my ma says about my pa, Baldy must have got up on the wrong side of the bed this morning."

"Which in his case is either side." Because Baldy's remark had been so cutting, I was trying to be funny, and at least JudyAnn smiled. "You going to try Eeek or Meek?"

"I don't know, Clue. Maybe we're interrupting something real important."

"Yeah." I did my best to sound serious. "Like maybe Eeek and Meek are the ones going to marry Baldy's big sisters, and they're meeting there to plan the wedding."

That time even Skipper grinned, for though an elderly thirteen, the Ribaldo twins were notoriously bashful—even in front of JudyAnn. "Could be, all right. The whole bunch of 'em look almighty serious, that's for sure. Come on. Let's go see if we can find some of the other fellers; ones that'll be a little more friendly."

There was something going on, all right. Everybody in town seemed to be out on the street, gathered in groups. And they were either shouting with excitement or engaged in serious discussions with each other, or running breathlessly from one group to another so they could be. It was strange, for everybody looked either wildly happy, dazed, or worried, and nobody seemed to have time for us. Finally, though, Skipper made a breakthrough.

"Hey, Pink," he shouted as he approached our sixth or seventh teammate, "what the dickens is going on? Why won't any of the fellows talk to us?"

"Who knows?" replied the boy we called Pink because his dog was an albino with pink eyes, hardly even turning around to see that it was Skipper who was questioning him. Heretofore Pink had practically worshipped Skipper, who Pink believed was one of maybe the two or three best first basemen in the country. He was always fetching things for Skipper because of it, running dumb little errands, and would have done practically anything the Skipper had asked.

"Well, then," Skipper pressed, ignoring Pink's uncharacteristic rudeness, "how come everybody but me and Clue missed our game?"

"I don't know!" our friend growled. "Maybe they all slept in. Or maybe baseball just ain't that important anymore. Now stop pestering me, Skipper. I'm trying to listen!"

"Stop pestering you! Pink, this is me! Skipper. I thought—"

"I said stop pestering me!" Pink, who never *ever* got mad, was actually glowering at Skipper. "I'm trying to learn how me and my ma are gonna be getting rich, and I can't concentrate with you jabbering behind me!"

Skipper recovered quickly from the massive dose of humility. "Getting rich? What're you talking about?"

"What do you think I'm talking about? Oil, that's what! Some feller's discovered a whole ocean of oil out under the Dome, and before long folks around here are going to be filthy rich on account of it!"

"What folks?"

"I . . . don't know, Skipper. Everybody, I guess. Leastwise the adults."

"My folks, too?" Skipper was incredulous.

"Yeah, everybody's folks, I reckon. Least that's what that geologist feller says."

"See?" JudyAnn intoned piously as Skipper turned back toward us. "Cluvarous didn't lie to you, Skipper. He wasn't making anything up, either." Proudly she lifted her head the way Mother sometimes did. "And neither was I. So there!"

But JudyAnn's rebuke was lost on the Skipper. "By jumpin' jehoshaphat, Clue," he breathed, getting more excited by the minute, "maybe that geologist feller that stayed with you last night really did find oil. Wouldn't that be something! I read in the paper about the folks in Pennsylvania and how they've all been getting rich off the oil they've drilled there. Whoopee and hot dog! Wouldn't that be something if it happened to us! To me and Ma and Pa and the little ones!"

Suddenly he stopped and looked at me, his eyes unnaturally wide. "Wow, Clue!" he breathed. "Since he came to your folks first, I'll bet purty soon you're going to be the richest family in town! No fooling! Richer, even, than the Pursemans!"

"Not likely," I grumbled as I kicked a dirt clod to smithereens. "Not if Pop has his way."

"Why not? What do you mean?"

"I mean that Pop says the Hurryups own that

Dome country, Skipper. Not us. Not anybody in town, for that matter." This time I kicked a rock with my boot, utterly disgusted. "He says that if anybody ever gets any money out of that oil, it'll be them."

"The Hurryups? Are you crazy? They're nothing but dumb Indians, for pete's sake!"

"Not according to Pop."

"Then your pop's crazier than you! They're Indians and we ain't, and your mother told us in school that Indians can't own land! I imagine that's especially true of crazy ones like the Hurryups. Just you wait and see!"

Unhappily I shook my head. "Mother may have said that, Skipper, but Father says the Hurryups have a deed recorded anyway. I heard him tell the geologist feller that, just last night—"

But Skipper was no longer listening. Instead he was off, his feet fairly flying as he sped toward his home with the news of impending wealth that would lift his father from the almost-poverty that Skipper called "miller-itis" and transform his family forever. JudyAnn and I kept going too, but not anywhere near as fast. Instead we poked along, listening to the news of the great oil strike as it spread like wildfire through our town, and wondering what it meant that none of our friends would speak to us any longer.

5

By the time JudyAnn and I got home, there were already people at the house, asking Father to open his recorder's office to get the legalities started. He had been explaining again and again about it being Saturday and the weekend of July Fourth, but so far his patient insistence had only turned their requests into demands. Finally, shortly after our return, he announced to the rapidly grow-ing crowd that a legal deed to the Dome and all the country around it had been recorded long before, but that the details surrounding the transaction were confidential and protected by law.

Within another hour there must have been fifty or sixty people in our yard—now angry more than frustrated—yelling that Father was a liar, that the Hurryups were Indians, and that Father was obligated by law to open his office and record a "legal" deed in the names of the townspeople.

"Zeke," a voice yelled loudly from the back of the crowd, "you weren't elected to stand in the way of progress and prosperity!"

"Or to stand up for them stinkin' Indians!" a woman shrieked.

"Way you're carrying on, Jones," another man shouted angrily, "it wouldn't surprise us if you were also the one that stopped the railroad from coming in here."

"Somebody else said the same thing!" a woman agreed, not even talking to Father any longer. As a matter of fact, few did, after that. They mostly yelled back and forth among themselves, as though Father were not even before them on the veranda.

"I can't imagine I never thought of that myself!"

"Zeke's desperate for power, folks say." It was the voice from the back of the crowd again. "That's why he ran for office. Next he'll want to be mayor, and then you can bet he'll go after the governor's office! This illegal deed he has filed for the Hurryups proves that he will stop at nothing!"

"Power's money!" chimed in somebody else. "A hundred dollars says he's got a private deal with them Injuns to split the money from all that oil!"

"He'll never split it with 'em, either, the greedy so-and-so! Give 'em a few trinkets and then send 'em packing. That's good enough for Indians, he'll say!"

"Jones is a liar!"

"A cheat!"

"A thief!"

"Now that he's got them miserable Hurryups in his pocket, there won't be any living with him!"

"Selfishness and greed!" the voice from the back shouted for the third time. And this time I heard the voice more clearly and noticed a certain stilted carefulness with the words. "You can see it in his eyes, that's certain. And like somebody already said, that fancy new horseless carriage he's got back there under wraps just goes to prove it!"

It was the geologist! Carlos was standing at the back of the crowd, egging the others on. Cautiously I looked to see him through the window, but couldn't for all the people.

"Is that what's under that canvas?" a woman yelled. "A horseless carriage? Well, at least he has the good sense to be ashamed of it!"

"He should be! Is that how you bought that fancy automobile, Zeke? With our money?"

"Probably is! He's been lording it over the rest of

us all high and mighty ever since he came to town fifteen years ago!"

"Yeah, but it's gotten worse since moneybags Purseman made him manager of his doggone bank."

"I always liked him, too, which goes to show I've been three kinds of a fool!"

"You and everybody else!"

"Do they think they're the Vanderbilts, for crying out loud?

"Or the Rockefellers?"

"I call it putting on airs, is what I call it."

"Well, that snooty Miss Abigail ain't no better'n him, coming all high and mighty with her fancy duds and piled-up hair, and putting on airs with her language and fancy talking the way she does."

"But, I thought she was a good teacher—"

"Good teacher? Harv, she's had you snookered with her pretty smile ever since kindeegarten, and you know it! If you ask me, the Joneses are both greedy social climbers, and they're teaching their two brats to be the same!"

At that I felt the blood rush in my ears, but as Mother's restraining arm held me still, I wondered that she and Father were remaining so calm. With all my heart I wanted to rush out there and tear into whoever was calling JudyAnn and me brats. Or maybe into the geologist himself, who was so busy stirring folks up against us.

"And like you said, Harriet," someone continued, "they're crooks to boot!"

"Maybe we ought to ride 'em all out of town on a rail!" This was Carlos again, turning the crowd like they were a boat and his hand was on the tiller.

"And give 'em a good warm coat of tar and feathers before we do!"

Everybody laughed at that—a dark, ugly-sounding laughter that sent chills straight through me. "Well," a man growled when it had ceased, "whether or not we have to tar and feather 'em, we will have that deed changed!"

"He's right!" another shouted. "Unless—hey, wait a minute! Without Zeke Jones around, the deed won't matter! Carlos said so, and I believe him! With Zeke gone, all that's keeping us from our money is them two crazy Injuns, and they can be got rid of easy as we do them jackrabbits out on the Dome."

"Yeah, we'll make them hurry up, all right!"

"Just like we're gonna do with the Joneses if they don't start acting like white folks again!"

"Where's Herm Pontius, for pete's sake?"

"Yeah! He's the gol-durned lawyer! Let's ask him about the best legal way to take back what's rightfully ours!"

"Herm's right over here, folks," Carlos shouted, "so ask away."

"Say, Herm? Tell us what we can do about these greedy so-and-so's that'll pass for legal—"

Father stood listening in silence as the hostile tide of public opinion rose ever more forcefully against him. JudyAnn and I sat on the floor just inside the door with Mother, also listening and growing more and more frightened. These people had been our friends, the people that Father had dealt with in the bank or that Mother had taught or met with in her clubs and civic groups. They were the parents of the fellows I played ball with. They were neighbors and acquaintances who would have done anything to help and support the rest of us— or so I had believed. But that had changed somehow, changed so fast that none of us could even imagine it.

Mother raised her hand and rubbed the side of her head time and time again that afternoon. As she hugged my sister and me to her bosom and huddled on the parlor floor listening to the crowd outside, I finally realized how much she was suffering.

With dark there were several fires burning at the edge of our yard and out in the road, and people were clustered around them carrying on intense, hushed conversations. Through one of the windows I caught sight of Carlos once, his lean figure looking elegant in the firelight, waxing eloquent with the dozen or so people gathered around him.

Later, the murmuring gave way to speechifying, and there were more chants and shouting, so that long after I had gone to bed I lay with my eyes wide open, staring at the flickering shadows on my ceiling and listening to the horrid things people were saying about our family and the Hurryups—

"Clue?"

Before I could stop her, JudyAnn had slid under the covers beside me.

"Get out of here!" I hissed angrily. "Don't you know girls ain't supposed to be in bed with boys?"

"Aren't," she corrected quietly. "Besides, I'm not being a girl right now. I'm just being your little sister, Cluvarous, and I'm scared."

"Yeah," I breathed as I relaxed and pulled the covers up over us so Mother wouldn't hear us. "Me too."

"Why are all those people so angry at us?"

I sighed. "Because Pop won't give them what they want."

"But Father doesn't own that land. The Hurryups do."

"Maybe. But Pop is the one who is letting them keep it. Pop's the one who says they ain't Indians."

"*Aren't,* Clue."

"Hey," I growled, "this is my bed! Remember?"

"That's your silliest excuse for bad grammer yet, Clue. Besides, it isn't like you don't know the right words."

"As if talking to dolls isn't silly?" I exploded, ignoring the last part of her statement. "Or playing house? Or making those stupid mud pies?"

"Sshhh," JudyAnn giggled. "You'll awaken the whole house. Besides, I'm just preparing to be a decent mother, modeling myself after the wonderful Abigail Jones, who is herself a perfect model of decency and propriety."

Hearing the personal twist on the airy speech that Mother had assigned all the girls in school to memorize, I couldn't help but laugh. "Mother *is* the perfect model, isn't she. And I don't know why I argue with her, Jude. I truly don't. Most everyone on earth sets store by all those proper manners and such, and I know Mother has my best interest at heart. At least she's told me so a thousand times. Yet sometimes it seems like so much nonsense that I feel I'm going to burst with it. I want to scream or shout or maybe even run down the street in my long johns yelling 'fire!' at the top of my lungs and watching everybody scurry for safety."

"Cluvarous! That's scandalous!"

I laughed quietly. "Maybe so, but sometimes that's how I feel!"

"Don't you want to be a philosopher like Father?" JudyAnn questioned in surprise. "I want to teach school like Mother."

"That's great for you, but Father thinks too much for me. I wouldn't like that. Besides, he's always reading those boring books and magazines. I like mysteries, and ghost stories, and true detective stories."

"And those horrid dime novels," JudyAnn added sarcastically. "You know what Mother says about them when she finds them in your room!"

"Humph!" I knew, all right, and I knew too well the punishment that always followed. The trouble was, I still enjoyed reading them—

"I guess you could grow up to be a baseball

player," JudyAnn declared hopefully. "They don't have to talk right."

"Oh, yeah! No matter how I talk, I'm so short nobody will even try to pitch to me, and I'm terrible at catching the ball."

"You can throw it real good."

That made me snort with derision. "Not compared to other fellers, I can't!"

"Well, you can throw it better than me, and I think that's real good."

"You're a girl, Jude. Girls ain't supposed to throw real good, because that ain't—"

"Isn't," JudyAnn corrected again.

"Yeah, isn't. Anyway, mothers and other grown-up female women don't ever have to throw real good, on account of nobody throws babies and other such stuff around. So it doesn't matter if girls can't throw. But men have to throw lots of things around, all their lives. Forks full of hay and manure, barrels of nails, sacks of grain, buckets of water—you name it. If a boy can't throw real good when he's small, then he can be in a terrible fix later on when folks are counting on him."

"I didn't know that, Clue."

"Well, me being older than you and all, there's lots of things you likely don't know that I do.

Maybe there's even things I don't know, but I doubt it. At least not very many."

"I know one thing you don't know."

"Oh, yeah? What's that, Miss Smartypants?"

"That isn't my name, Clu*Various!*"

"And my name's Clue," I retorted angrily. "So, what is it you know that I don't?"

"Oh, not very much. I just know that if you didn't argue with Mother all the time, you'd be better off. You're always going after her. And now this thing with Father—making him feel badly about sticking up for the Hurryups. Sometimes I think you hate them, Clue."

"Who?" I was surprised that JudyAnn would think such a thing. "Mother and Father?"

"Of course. The way you talk sometimes, that's how it sounds."

Thoughtfully I wiggled my toes against the sheets, subconsciously enjoying the feeling of the cool fabric against my skin. Hate our parents? Of course I didn't. In fact, I was proud as punch of them, and gloried in the distinction of being their son. I wanted them to be proud of me, too. It was just that lately I had different ideas about things than they did, like about Carlos and the money and the whole town hating us.

"Maybe that's why Mother has sick headaches," JudyAnn declared abruptly as she pulled herself out of my bed and slipped to the floor.

"And just what is that supposed to mean?"

"I just think you should listen more, Clue. Father and Mother need us to stand beside them. I'll bet they're just as scared as us. I'm tired now, so I'm going back to my own bed. Okay?"

Before I knew what she was doing, JudyAnn bent over and gave me a little kiss. "Goodnight," she said through a sudden yawn, and then she headed for the door.

"Goodnight," I mumbled in return, and in wonder I wiped dry my cheek.

6

Sunday morning found me poorly rested but relieved that everybody was gone from our yard. As I walked around looking at the dead fires and scattered debris, I wondered if they had gone because it was the Sabbath or simply because they had run out of stuff to burn.

When I came back in I found Mother up and bustling around, and soon she was feeding us and getting us all ready for worship services just as she did every Sunday morning. And at the appointed hour we were seated in our regular pew at the church, preparing to sing the first hymn of the day.

Everything seemed so normal to me that morning, so much the same as every other Sunday. The sun was bright and warm, the stained glass window on the east of the building was casting prisms of color throughout the room, and folks were all scrubbed clean and dressed in their Sunday best. Yet there was a feeling in the air that was impossible to miss—a sense of anger or hostility directed toward Father and the rest of us that made me want to duck under the pew and hide. Everywhere I looked, people were glaring at us, and even my teammates offered me no smiles, no offhand waves of greeting.

The Reverend Mr. Sumsion preached that day on the Lord delivering the Promised Land to the Israelites because the former inhabitants were wicked and not the Lord's people. He was glowering directly at Father as he preached that sermon, and at its conclusion he added a postscript about elected officials being required by their oaths of office to be their brothers' keeper. I don't know about JudyAnn, but I understood fairly well what the Reverend was saying, and I'm sure Father and Mother understood his message even better than I did.

There was an eerie silence afterward as we all filed out of the church, something I had never before experienced. So far as I can remember, not one person in that congregation hugged or shook hands with us the way folks usually did. By the same token, neither did they shake hands with each other. I suppose they were too busy trying to stare Father down, endeavoring by the power of their individual and collective wills to force him into changing his mind. Unfortunately, they didn't know him as well as they thought they did.

"Well, Abby darling," Father sighed when at last we were safely home, "it looks like we've got ourselves into a pickle."

"No, Ezekiel," Mother declared as she unpinned her hat and tossed it onto the settee, "the man called Carlos has created the pickle, and he needed no help from us. Was he there today, in church?"

"I didn't see him."

"Neither did I, but I have no doubt that he is around somewhere." Suddenly she smiled. "You know, he reminds me of a flea, which is the dishonest politician of the insect world. More and more it looks like Carlos is the perfect human example of the same." Now she was making no attempt to hide the disgust in her voice. "Both he and the flea are constantly itching for place, they create no end of disturbance and turmoil, and no one ever knows exactly where to find either one of them!"

"Flea or not," Father chuckled, "you can tell he's a politician, all right. Most of them only stand for what they think others will fall for, and Carlos is no exception."

Now both my parents were laughing, a condition that had been scarce in our home of late, and JudyAnn and I were happy to join the brief moment of levity.

"What I don't understand," Mother continued, suddenly serious again, "are his motives. I keep asking myself why he is doing this, turning the town so against us, and for the life of me I can't think it through."

"In my opinion," Father responded gravely while JudyAnn and I climbed into our favorite over-stuffed chairs to await the end of the discussion and our dinner, "it is about power—both for Carlos and for his company."

"But why didn't he just wait until next Tuesday when you'll be back in your office, and let the law take care of the Hurryups?"

Father smiled patiently. "Don't you see, my dear? What if he's wrong about them? He is no doubt asking himself what he will do if they really aren't Indians—as both they and I claim—and their deed to the Dome turns out to be legal and binding. And what if they aren't interested in selling—to him or anybody else?"

Abruptly Father turned and walked to the window, his hands thrust firmly into his jacket pockets. "The other day I was reading an article by Ida M. Tarbell, the muckraker, concerning a large eastern firm whose business practices are based upon a corporate policy of selfishness and greed. She gave numerous examples of blackmail, confiscation of property, and every other business vice occurring at all levels of the corporation. Her point was that if business is to be treated as warfare and not as a peaceful pursuit, they cannot expect their adversaries to lie down and die without a fight."

Turning back toward us, Father's look was fiercely determined. "So it is with me! The vicious, corrupt way we have been attacked merely strengthens my resolve to defend the Hurryups and their deed to the last! Yes, and that in spite of every threat that Carlos de Ortega or anybody else can generate against me. It matters not what things they falsely accuse me of. What matters is what I do, Abby, and I will do what I know to be right!"

Mother was shaken. "But . . . but what will happen?"

Slowly Father shook his head. "I don't know, sweetheart. I just don't know."

He grew silent, deep in thought as he again

turned to the window, and so Mother arose and went into the kitchen. Soon she was back with a tray of cookies and, unbelievably, four steaming mugs of her expensive European chocolate.

"I know this is early," she said with a warm smile as she handed us the mugs, "but since we seem to be having a family progress meeting, we might as well enjoy our treats at the same time."

"Quite right," Father declared as he took his mug from Mother and began sipping at it. JudyAnn and I were doing the same, savoring and doing our best to prolong each delicious taste of that exquisite chocolate. I had even managed to push from my mind the gist of our family conversation in favor of enjoying my drink, and so was taken by surprise when Father turned to me.

"My question now is, can each of you support my decision to defend the Hurryups' deed? If I do, it's bound to affect all of us in one way or another, and we'll have to be prepared to deal with whatever comes. Cluvarous, what do you have to say?"

Well, I was stumped. In spite of all Father had said about the rightness of things, I hadn't enjoyed having my friends ostracize me the past couple of days. And I truly had been looking forward to a life of wealth. Besides which, there was Mother's unwavering conviction that the Hurryups were Indian—

"I don't know, Pop," I finally responded. "I still think that maybe you should give the people what they want. I mean, the Hurryups are definitely strange, maybe even crazy. Everybody knows that. And when I saw them up close, they sure looked like Indians to me." I punctuated my answer with another sip of my chocolate.

"Very well, Clue," Father responded after a long moment of simply looking at me, making me terribly uncomfortable. "You're telling me that rather than helping to see the Hurryups through this crisis, you can now see through them. You are convinced they are liars and thieves, not at all who they represent themselves to be. Therefore, your vote is for me to submit to the will of the people despite the fact that it may be not only wrong but illegal, and take from the Hurryups all that they have spent their lives acquiring."

Hesitantly I nodded, for I knew full well that he was forcing me to remember Mother's saying. Still, I couldn't shed the thought of how wonderful it would be to have a bunch of money and be back in the good graces of the town—back on the baseball diamond with my friends.

"Thank you. I'll take that into consideration." Next he turned to my sister. "JudyAnn, do you have any thoughts on the matter?"

"I like the Hurryups," she replied simply, brightly. "Do you know why, Father? The Hurry- ups smiled at Clue down at the ball field, and they talked to him and shook his hand. I couldn't hear what they said, but I saw them smile, and I think they're nice."

"So, your vote is to defend their deed as fully legal?" Father pressed, pretending not to notice the discomfort my sister's words had caused me. I was troubled because of the Hurryups, because of my own memories of them. They *had* been nice to me, and I knew it.

JudyAnn smiled and shrugged at Father's second question, and we all knew she had said all she intended to say.

"Abby, it's your turn. What do you think I should do?"

Mother was silent for some time—so long, in fact, that I thought maybe she hadn't heard. She was staring at her hands, which were folded in her lap, and I found myself wondering if a person could go to sleep with her eyes open. But when she looked up at Father I saw the tears brimming on her lower eyelids, and I knew she had not been asleep at all.

"Ezekiel, if you are really going to push the issue about the Hurryups not being Indian, then I *must* know what makes you so certain!"

Softly Father sighed. "Abby, you know that is confidential."

Quickly Mother shook her head. "That isn't good enough, darling, not today. The children and I have always trusted you, for each of us knows you love us and would never deceive us. But today, at least, we need a little more than trust. Those people outside are getting angry enough to be dangerous. To help you stand against them, we need information."

"But, I can't—"

"You've already admitted to us and everybody else in town that there is a deed in the Hurryups' name," Mother interrupted, "which I believe is also confidential information. Are you certain you can't tell us this one additional detail?"

Soberly Father regarded Mother, and it was easy to tell that his mind was in a turmoil. Finally, though, he smiled, and for some reason I breathed a sigh of relief.

"You know, I don't think the Hurryups would

mind if I told you. In fact, they've been talking for years about putting something in Spots Heyermier's paper about their past, as well as their gratitude for the friendship of the community. So my telling you this one more detail shouldn't bother them much at all."

Stepping away from the parlor window, Father cradled his mug in his hands. "Shortly after my first election, Gabriel—that's Mr. Hurryup's name—came in to record the deed to his land. Part of it he had homesteaded years and years ago, and he had the government documents to prove it. The other part he had purchased from a rancher who had proved up on the land in the late 1850s. Gabriel, of course, had a bill of sale from him for every square foot of what he had purchased. Naturally I combined them and recorded Gabriel's deed of ownership."

"But all that will mean nothing if he is an Indian—"

Father nodded as he sat down beside Mother. "Gabriel also brought with him that day an old family Bible—a *very old* family Bible that was not even printed in English. In it was recorded a genealogy of his family, going back, as I recollect, ten generations. Some of the names I was unable to read, and so Gabriel read them to me, explaining that they had been recorded in a script called Gaelic, the ancient Celtic language of Scotland and Ireland."

Mother appeared shocked. "Are you saying—"

"That's right, darling. Gabriel's name was the last one to be recorded, and he was born in Scotland, the son of a very well-known clan leader whose name I swore never to reveal."

"Ezekiel—"

Father shrugged. "That's all I intend to say, Abby, so it will do no good to press me further. But tell me, when was the last time you heard about an Indian of any sort being born Scottish, in Scotland, and of a famous Scottish clan?"

Mother's face was a picture. "So he's Scottish? And you believe his Bible is authentic?"

"We accept such records as proof of birth. One of our state statutes provides for it."

Now Mother sighed deeply and her shoulders slumped, as though all the starch had been taken out of her. "Very well. I suppose I am satisfied." For a moment or two the room was silent, and I think we were all feeling a little despair. Then Mother straightened, squared her shoulders again, gave Father a quick smile, and looked at us. "Do you children have any further questions?"

"What about Mrs. Hurryup?" I asked hopefully, still thinking of the money. "Is she an Indian?"

"I don't think so, Clue. But it wouldn't matter if she were. You see, the deed is recorded in the name of Gabriel, not his wife, Keziah Jane, and he is most definitely entitled to legal ownership of the Dome country."

"Anything else?" Mother pressed as she looked at JudyAnn and then me.

And neither of us said anything at all.

7

It was well after dark when someone threw the first rock. It was a poor throw, however, clattering across our veranda but doing no damage that I could discern. Since late afternoon we had been hearing occasional voices coming from out in the yard, but though all of us had looked out the window from time to time, there had been no sign of the crowd we had put up with the night before.

As evening descended, Mother had decided to leave our lamps unlit, so we had all been sitting around listening as Father played song after song on our spinet, the darkness not bothering him at all.

That first rock was followed by a second and then a third in rapid succession, and it was the third one that shattered one of the panes in our big parlor window.

"Cluvarous," Mother ordered from the doorway behind us, her voice low but urgent, "you take JudyAnn and get upstairs! Now!"

"Yes, Mother," I responded as my sister and I pulled quickly back and rose to our feet. My heart was suddenly pounding in my chest, and for the first time in my life I felt a fear that I might actually die.

"Clue," Father said from the spinet seat as we started up the stairs, "wait a moment."

"Yes, Father?"

"This could get ugly." Father's voice was filled with worry. "I hope it doesn't, but in case something happens to your mother or me, you take JudyAnn out the back door and get into the hills. In the morning, if we haven't come for you, take your sister and go straight to the Hurryups—"

"The Hurryups!" Mother exclaimed in surprise. "But Zeke—"

"Abby, think about it. Do you know anyone else we can trust? I mean with absolute certainty?"

"I . . . I suppose not," she replied quietly, and even the darkness could not hide her bleak resignation.

"All right, son." Father was still seated at the

spinet. "Do as I've told you, and I promise that things will work out."

"Can we get to the Dome that way?"

"Yes," Father nodded, "you can. That's the way the Hurryups usually come and go, so I'm sure there must be some sort of trail. Just work your way south, and either you'll find the trail or the Hurryups will find you."

I nodded my understanding, limited as it was, and together JudyAnn and I scrambled up the stairs and into my bedroom. We were hardly there when I heard the front door open and then slam closed again, so I hurried to the window and looked down. To my everlasting surprise, Mother was standing alone on the steps of the veranda below us, holding high a lantern and peering out into the darkness.

"Who's there?" she called out fearlessly.

There was a slight rustling in our bushes, and another rock clattered against the porch.

"Jimmy Newsome," Mother called, "is that you? You always were one for hiding out and then throwing rocks at the girls. Too bad somebody didn't tan your hide but good—teach you some proper manners! Jimmy, you answer me!"

There was the sound of hoarse whispering, but no answer.

"Of all the ridiculous behavior!" Mother continued. "Whoever you are, you must surely know that the Sabbath is no day for contention. I taught you that, and I wager your own mothers did too!" Mother's free hand was rubbing the side of her head as she tried to peer out beyond the lantern light. "John Scat, you're another rock thrower. Is that you out in those bushes? Make yourself known, before we send for Sheriff McCabe!"

Without warning several tomatoes came flying onto the veranda, one hitting the doorpost and another hitting Mother in the shoulder. She gasped, apparently more in surprise than pain, and the next thing I knew, Father was out the door and standing in front of her, my new baseball bat held threateningly in his hand.

"You get along now, you hear?" He was holding my bat out in front of him as he descended the stairs, shaking it in the direction of our bushes like a stick. "If you have something to say, you sniveling cowards, spit it out! Otherwise get out of here, every one of you, before I lose my temper!"

I couldn't see Father's face, but his expression must have been something fierce. There was another rustling in the bushes and the furious pounding of feet as several individuals fled toward town. Only when no further sound was heard did Father turn and mount the steps to Mother, put his arm around her, and lead her back into the house.

8

"Abby, my darling, are you certain you're all right? Here, let me clean this mess off you—"

While JudyAnn and I crowded to the top of the stairs, Father hung the lantern and tenderly began cleaning remnants of tomato from Mother's shoulder, arm, and chest.

"I am perfectly all right!" Mother declared forcefully as she stood with hands clenched at her sides.

"I guess there's no telling how low some people will stoop," Father breathed as he collected bits of tomato into his hand. "Throwing tomatoes at a woman, for pity's sake! I'm of a mind to go down to my office right now and remove that blasted deed before somebody tries to remove it for me!"

"I will not be bullied by the likes of that mob!" Mother was seething—actually trembling, she was so upset. "I simply will not!"

Then, just as in the kitchen that night when Carlos had first come to our house, her hand went to her temple, a look of pain and confusion crossed her face, her knees abruptly gave way, and she seemed to melt toward the floor. This time, though, Father was prepared, and he scooped her into his arms so quickly that I don't think even her skirts touched the floor.

"Kids," he ordered softly as he started up the stairs toward us, "let's get into JudyAnn's room. It's in the back and should be safer."

JudyAnn and I fled down the hall. Father came behind us carrying Mother, and soon she was comfortably positioned on JudyAnn's bed, So-Help-Me Hannah's knitted afghan—a gift to our family the previous Christmas—spread over her.

"There," Father soothed as he wiped Mother's face with a damp cloth JudyAnn had brought in, "you'll be just fine now, Abby-girl."

Mother tried to smile. "You . . . you haven't called me that in a long time."

"Haven't I? Well, I certainly meant to." Father then turned to me. "Clue, would you please go down and put out the lantern, and then light candles in your room and ours? That's a boy."

In less than two minutes I was back, and it didn't seem to me that any of my family had even moved.

"Thank you, Cluvarous." Father smiled at me. "Now, I think you and JudyAnn have experienced enough excitement for one evening—"

"But what about Mother?" JudyAnn asked worriedly.

"She'll be just fine," Father responded as he stroked Mother's forehead. "All she needs is rest, just like the two of you. JudyAnn, why don't you use our bed—"

"Zeke," Mother said as she reached out and took JudyAnn by the hand, "don't send them away—not yet. This is no time for them to be sent alone into those front rooms."

Soberly Father nodded. "You're right, Abby-girl. I hadn't thought of that."

Mother smiled wanly. "Besides, I'm not ready to see them go, either. Come, children, and sit here beside me."

"Aren't you feeling well, Mother?" JudyAnn was anxious.

"JudyAnn, don't you worry about your mother. It'll take more than a tomato on my blouse to make me flinch—at least a puny little tomato like that one. Say, did I ever tell you and Cluvarous about your grandmother's tomatoes? The ones she grew when she was a girl?"

"Is this the grandma who didn't have shoes to wear to school?" JudyAnn asked excitedly.

"That's right," Mother smiled. "Would you like to hear the story?"

Eagerly we both nodded, and Father sat so that he could hold Mother's head in his lap. Our grandmother had died when Mother was just a girl, and so she didn't often speak of her. But when she did, it was always like a secret—something private that we didn't spread around to others.

Besides that, I loved to listen to Mother's stories no matter what their topic, for she had a gift for making the characters become so alive that I seemed actually to see them in my mind. Of course, during the previous few months there hadn't been many stories, what with my arguing and her sick headaches and all. So this was going to be a treat—

"This is the way she told it to me," Mother began, "one time when I was feeling sad. Of course, you can never tell with stories, but your grandmother swore that every word of it was true."

There was something distant about Mother as she spoke that night—maybe the candlelight or something. She was looking right at JudyAnn and me, but she seemed to be looking at something else, too.

"There wasn't much money in your grandmother's home," she continued, "but that doesn't mean they weren't blessed. For a fact, her father had settled on some of the most fertile ground in the whole country, and Mother used to say that if a stranger passed through the area and spoke highly of some other place, every beet got red in the face, every potato winked its eye, every oat field was shocked, the rye heads all stroked their beards, the corn pricked up its ears, and every foot of ground started kicking. That's how every living thing felt about that wonderful country."

Well, JudyAnn was listening all serious-like, but Father was grinning, and I was trying to believe my ears. Just what sort of story was this—

"One of their best crops during those times," Mother went on, "were sunflowers, which grew so big they used to chop the stalks up for firewood or use them for railroad ties. They also held family picnics under the shade of the taller ones, though first they had to fire off shotguns to frighten away the flocks of crows that liked to roost in their branches. Once one of your grandmother's neighbors made the mistake of tying her cow to a growing sunflower while she went to get her milk pail, and by the time she got back, her poor cow was dangling twenty feet in the air.

"One day a rattlesnake bit a sunflower stalk on the property of another neighbor, and the stalk swelled so big he had it chopped down and milled, and then he built his family a new house out of the lumber. Unfortunately, when he painted it, the turpentine in the paint took out all the swelling, and the poor man ended up having to use the new place for a birdhouse."

"Mother—"

"Don't worry, Cluvarous," Mother smiled as she reached down and took my hand, "I'm getting to those tomatoes."

"I know," I argued, startled that she had taken my hand but very much soothed by the pleasant, comfortable feel of it. "But—"

"One day when she was out playing in the back forty acres," Mother quickly continued, "she found a dried tomato that was chock full of seeds, so she planted them on the spot and went on with her play. A few weeks later her father asked her to find a lost sow pig and her shoats, and in searching your grandmother came onto the place where she had planted the tomato seeds.

"Imagine her surprise when she saw tomato vines as tall as a young hickory tree, and thick enough she could use them for bridges over the numerous ravines she had to cross as she continued her search. She didn't find the pigs that day, but she did find green tomatoes that were practically as big as herself.

"All summer she looked for those lost pigs, and every time she passed through the back forty she checked on her tomato vines, which by fall had reached horrendous size. And with the vines that large, it doesn't take much to imagine how huge her tomatoes were getting to be.

"Then one day as she was climbing through the vines that now filled the back forty, still searching for her father's lost pigs, she heard a funny noise coming from inside one of her monstrous tomatoes. Going back for an axe, she chopped an opening in the side of the tomato and discovered the sow and her shoats. Early in the summer the tomato had apparently lost part of its skin being scraped along the ground by its fast-growing vine. The pigs had chewed themselves inside at the scrape, and they had been living off tomato pulp and juice ever since, all fat and happy and shielded from the weather. In fact, the shelter was so good that her father allowed the pigs to use it through the winter, and then he turned two of her larger tomatoes into a barn and outbuildings."

While Father sat caressing Mother's hair and chuckling, Mother looked down at JudyAnn and me and winked. "Now, children, *those* are tomatoes that might make me flinch!"

9

"Mother, we've got to hurry!" I was shouting as I bounded down the stairs, frantically trying to do up my buttons. It was the next morning, July Fourth, and somehow I had slept in. The traumatic events of the weekend, so large in my mind until Mother's silly story of the tomatoes, were already a thing of the past. It was now the morning of a new day, and I couldn't wait to get on with the celebration.

A sudden *bang* rattled the windowpanes of our house, and Mother grabbed the back of a chair to steady herself. "What was that?" she cried as a second explosion followed the first.

"That's Doc Bones firing off the Civil War cannon," I shouted enthusiastically, "just the way he did it during the war! Hear it? There's the third, and in a minute it will be four explosions, for 1904.

Gee whiz, Mother, the shindig's already started! We've got to get going!"

Sitting alone in the parlor, Mother, looking exhausted, smiled wanly. "I know you have slept in, Cluvarous, but I allowed it. Your Father asked us all to stay home today, and I think we'd better do as he says."

I was stunned. *"Stay home?* But, Mother—"

Automatically she held up her hand. "No arguments, Cluvarous. JudyAnn is in the kitchen waiting breakfast, and I would appreciate it if you would join her."

"But there's a free community breakfast, with all sorts of good stuff that we hardly ever have. And after that there's going to be horse races and foot races and a big watermelon roll—"

"Cluvarous!"

"Yes, Mother," I sighed with dejection, knowing the argument was over. "Where's Father?"

"He's gone to the bank to get that deed to the Dome."

"But if he can go out, then surely it'll be safe for the rest of us. Please, Mother, it's a holiday!"

"Cluvarous, I know what day this is. I also know you are not to leave this house. Is that clear? Now, JudyAnn is waiting for you. Though her food is growing cold, she insisted." In spite of her exhaustion, Mother's look was firm, and I knew she was not going to be answering any more questions.

Grumbling under my breath, I headed for the kitchen and my obnoxious little sister. This was crazy! Why would Father want us to miss such a grand celebration? Games, the parade, orations, the reading of the Declaration of Independence, a variety show, a dance, even fireworks! I couldn't stand to miss all of that! I had been counting on it for too long!

"Cluvarous," JudyAnn called as I marched resolutely toward the back door and my escape to the big doings in town, "where are you going? I've been waiting almost half an hour so we could eat together."

"Yeah," I growled in passing, "and you can keep waiting, for all I care!"

"But Mother even made flapjacks!"

"I don't care, JudyAnn! I'm not going to miss—"

"*Abigail! Abigail Jones, come quickly!*"

It was So-Help-Me Hannah screeching, and she hadn't even bothered to wait for Mother to open the front door. She had simply knocked and then burst in, and her red face and heaving chest told Mother that she was seriously anxious about something.

Without thought I spun about and hurried to the inner door, not even realizing that JudyAnn was beside me, hanging fearfully onto my arm.

"Abigail—"

"Merciful heavens, Hannah," Mother replied as she rose hurriedly from the settee, "what is it?"

"Ezekiel's in trouble," our neighbor panted, at the same time gesturing with her hand toward town. "He . . . he . . . They have him surrounded!"

"Who has him surrounded? What are you talking about?"

"Oh, Abigail," and now So-Help-Me Hannah abandoned all attempts at Mother's cherished protocol, "it's practically the whole crazy town, is who. They have Zeke and the bank surrounded, Mr. Purseman isn't there to help him, and now the crowd's shouting awful, terrible threats against him!"

"But . . . but what started it again?"

"Lawsy, Abigail, you know perfectly well what started it! Carlos and his money! He's been going about since way before daylight, filling folks' heads so full of visions of gold and silver that they believe the money's already theirs, and Zeke has somehow managed to steal it. This morning, though, Carlos has thrown down the gauntlet. He says the town has until tomorrow night to free up the Dome so his company can go to drilling. Otherwise he's taking his money and going elsewhere. When Zeke came by the bank this morning, they were waiting for him. Oh, Abigail, that geologist has folks so stirred up that I . . . I'm afraid there's going to be a lynching!"

"A lynching?" Mother breathed the word slowly, and I could actually see the color drain from her face. "Oh, mercy, Hannah! I must get down there! Can you get word to Sheriff McCabe?"

"No need to," the woman replied scornfully. "He's there—in the crowd. I saw him take off his badge a little bit ago and put it in his pocket. Mayor Frost's there too, and all he did was grin! I . . . I thought the best thing I could do was to come and warn you."

"Thank you, Hannah." Looking stricken, Mother raised her hand to the side of her head and began to massage her left temple. But then, abruptly, she dropped her hand and her head came erect. "Very well," she declared, her shoulders squaring again just as they had the evening before, "Zeke and I will face these dear friends and neighbors of ours together! He's in the right, and right will most certainly prevail!

"Clue," she said as she quickly pinned her newest hat in place, surprising me with her use of my treasured nickname, "you remember what your father told you yesterday evening? Take JudyAnn. Go through the hills. And go now!"

Bending over, Mother kissed each of us and held us to her bosom. Then she released us and stood, and without another word she walked past the frightened So-Help-Me Hannah and out the door, striding down off the veranda and toward the center of town. And instead of being obedient and heading for the Hurryups like both our parents had instructed me, I grabbed JudyAnn's hand, gave what I hoped was a withering glare at our cowardly neighbor because she had not accompanied Mother, and followed after.

10

Mother turned neither to the right nor to the left as she marched down the road, but went with eyes straight forward and head held high, almost as though she were defying the world to try to stop her. Meanwhile, JudyAnn and I were stumbling and running and stumbling again, doing all we could to keep up with her.

Because we were all going so fast, we soon began passing little knots of people who were also going in our direction—going, I thought at first, to the community breakfast and Independence Day celebration. But right away I started hearing the vilest sorts of things being said about my parents and the Hurryups, and I knew I had been wrong. The only thing those people were celebrating was the terrible poison Carlos had somehow infused into their thinking! That and some of the things they intended to do to my parents so that "justice" could be served.

I'm certain Mother must have heard the remarks as well, but if she did, she gave no sign of it. She simply continued, letting the insults and threats bounce off without effect. To me she seemed regal at that moment, like a princess or a queen. She was more elegant than any Gibson girl ever drawn— more elegant, even, than Alice Roosevelt herself! I felt so proud of her, so proud to be her son, that I couldn't keep from bawling. Naturally JudyAnn was crying too.

We were just passing the livery stable and freight office, a block north of the post office and still two blocks from the bank, when a sudden shout made JudyAnn and me stop in our tracks. I turned to look just in time to see a fist-sized rock leave somebody's hand. It seemed to hang in the air for a moment. I watched it but for some reason could not find voice to shout a warning. Then it hit with a solid *thwump,* striking Mother exactly on her left temple. Like an empty dress she crumpled silently into the road, and there she lay without moving.

I heard a yell of triumph from someone, another person cursed something awful, and someone else shouted that the snooty teacher was down and that her lying, thieving husband was going to be next. But I didn't see the owners of those angry voices, at least not distinctly. Instead, I was at my mother's side, looking down in horror at her still form in the dirt of the road and at the growing lump and trickle of blood on the side of her lovely face. That was all I could see, and all I could hear was the screaming of my mind, trying to make sense of what I had just seen.

For some reason then I happened to glance up, and though a crowd was gathering around us I looked through and past them and saw only one man, standing to the side of the freight office with his arms folded resolutely. Then I knew, and from that moment I had eyes for no one else. It was Carlos de Ortega, of course, and he had won! Even though he may not have thrown the rock, Carlos had had his revenge against Father. Mother lay motionless in the street, and no one seemed to care.

"You dirty coward!" I shrieked as I grabbed up handsful of earth and clods and began throwing them wildly in his direction. "You murdering liar! I hate you! I'll get you for this! I swear I will!" My voice was high and shrill, and I was probably making no sense to anyone but me. But I meant every word, and I wanted Carlos to know it. Somehow, somewhere, I was going to get even with that man—

Everything after that became a sort of red haze, like an endless nightmare from which I could not awaken. I kept my eyes glued on the evil Carlos, I think believing that if I looked away, he would somehow escape from me. I may even have continued screaming at him. I don't know. I can't remember.

I believe that quite a few people stopped and looked down at Mother before hurrying on, and one or two of them may even have knelt for a moment beside her, feeling for her pulse. That's fuzzy. But then somehow Mother spoke to me, clearly and distinctly, the fuzziness ended, and I remember what followed as if it had been uttered only moments ago.

"Clue," I was certain I heard her say, her voice sounding calm and serene even though her lips were not moving. "Cluvarous, dear, look at me."

I did not want to tear my eyes from the face over by the freight office. I had to keep glaring at him—

"Cluvarous, darling. Please."

Unable to resist any longer, I looked down and then dropped to my knees beside JudyAnn and my mother. Her eyes were closed and she looked just as she had a moment or so before—utterly lifeless. Yet I swear that she spoke to me again.

"My dear, strong Cluvarous," she declared, and her voice was as soothing as cool water on a hot afternoon, "please don't waste your emotions, your wonderful passion—"

"But, Mother—" I began to argue.

"Cluvarous, darling," she interrupted, her voice so calm and quiet that I had to be still in order to hear, "you have so much good in you, and you must use it for good. Be proud of who you are and live to help others, and I promise that you will be well-loved—a happy man.

"Remember," she seemed to continue, though I could see clearly that there was still no movement of her lips, no least flicker of her long, dark eyelashes, "only your grandmother ever grew tomatoes big enough to make a person flinch."

"I . . . I'll remember!"

"I'm sure you will. That's one of the reasons why I love you so dearly. Now, please do what your father told you last evening. Take JudyAnn, go through the hills, and go now!"

Having no idea of how she had been speaking to me, but for some reason not finding it a bit strange or unusual, I felt myself being galvanized into action. "Come on," I yelped at my little sister while people continued to stream past, most paying little or no attention to us or Mother's still form. "We've got to get out of here!"

Quickly I ducked through the crowd and darted down the alley beside the livery stable, JudyAnn stumbling after. Somehow we got across the creek and into the willows on the far side, and the next clear memory I have is of dragging my sobbing sister over some rock formations in the hills that rolled along between the east side of our town and the Dome. After that I don't remember a thing—not one single detail until a long time later, when I found myself on my back in the dirt, staring up into the fierce blue eyes of Gabriel Hurryup.

PART TWO

11

"Howdy-do, Cluvarious Ezekiel Jones! Howdy-do, and what doings be these? Ye look as though ye've been to yonder hills and back, and fought the Rickaree whilst ye were there. Aye, and maybe lost your topknot in the bargain. Who might be the wee thing that be clinging to ye? Laws a'mercy! Might this be the sweet Miss JudyAnn?"

Groggily I sat up, and was amazed to find that it was nearly sunset and that my little sister was sleeping soundly beside me, our hands still locked together. Somehow we had not become separated, and so it was together that Gabriel Hurryup had found us.

"It . . . is JudyAnn," I croaked, the pain in my throat reminding me of the terrible thirst that had been plaguing me for what seemed forever. "Our

107

mother, Abigail Jones, she . . . she has been murdered—"

"Murdered, is it?" The man seemed saddened more than shocked, and I wondered at that. "Well, lad, if that be true, 'tis sorry I be for the both of ye. Your father spoke wondrous kindly of her, and ye younguns will be missing her something fierce. Does your father yet live?"

"I . . . I don't know. That's where Mother was going when she was hit by that rock. So-Help-Me Hannah, she said—"

"Wagh!" Gabriel Hurryup spat, suddenly upset. "Don't ye be cursing now, laddie! Cursing be a bad habit for anyone to get into, most of all a youngun of your fine upbringing."

"I . . . I'm not cursing," I stammered, surprised and wondering even more. "So-Help-Me Hannah is what folks call our neighbor, Hannah Tewksberry. She told us that the mob had Father surrounded, and that they were maybe going to kill him on account of he wouldn't say you were Indian or tear up your deed to the Dome."

"Ahh," Gabriel Hurryup breathed as if he now understood everything perfectly. "So that be the way their sticks float, be it? Well, lad, them be bad doings, that's certain." For a moment he said nothing, but simply stared off into the distance, apparently lost in thought. I was thinking too, remembering with a growing sense of anger that this strange-talking man was as much at the bottom of all our troubles as was Carlos. If Father hadn't been trying to protect him and his probably illegal deed, then Mother would still be alive and JudyAnn and I would still be—

"'Tis thirsty ye'll be," Gabriel Hurryup suddenly declared, glaring down at me. "Thing of it be, there be no water in miles. Fact is, this here'd be a fine country if only we had good water. But then, by jingo, so would hell!" Throwing back his head, he began laughing at his own poor joke, a strange cackle that nearly unnerved me, it was so odd. "Lad," he declared, abruptly serious again, "ye can drink till ye founder once we're at the home place. But ye'll have to get there on your own, for I'll be packing along this sweet little vision of loveliness. Be ye up to it, do ye think?"

"I'm up to whatever you can throw at me!" I snarled as my anger at this crazy-talking Indian boiled higher. I was absolutely determined to keep up with his famous rapid stride no matter how thirsty I felt, and I wanted him to know it.

Seeming not to notice my attitude, the strange

fellow hoisted the still-sleeping JudyAnn into his arms. To my amazement, though, he did not seem to be in a particular hurry, but walked slowly enough that I had no difficulty keeping up. Yet he moved as smoothly as an Indian, his beaded moccasins toeing in instead of out like my feet did— exactly the way one of my dime novels had said Indians walked—and making no sound on the hard, rocky ground.

Carlos had been right all along. The Hurryups had pulled the wool over Father's eyes with their tales of Scottish clans and their old book—which wasn't even in a language Father could read. How could he know it was a Bible, and that those dates in the front weren't scribbles put there by the old Indian himself?

Mother had died for nothing. And perhaps Father had died too, I thought grimly as I followed Gabriel Hurryup through a region of rocks and up a long, gradual rise of ground. Somehow, I determined, I was going to expose this man for what he was! A living, breathing Indian! Maybe I couldn't bring my mother back, but if Father was still alive, I could at least show him how wrong he had been. After that, I continued to vow, I would find a way to go after the evil Carlos—

For an hour we walked, maybe more, and the country was all barren and hilly. Occasionally there were patches of dry grass and brush, and low-growing junipers were scattered about. But the land was anything but green and fertile. Gabriel Hurryup had been right about the water. Nowhere did I ever see any sign of it, and again and again I found myself wondering why anyone—even a crazy Indian—would want to file claim to such a desolate country. It had to be because of oil—

Finally Gabriel Hurryup, still carrying JudyAnn, led me down a steep hill and into the small pocket or swale on the side of the Dome where he had built his cabin. It didn't seem to be much of a cabin, either. Surrounded by empty pole corrals (to this day I don't know where he had managed to find those poles) that were rotted and sagging in places and falling to the earth, the cabin looked to have been built a very long time before, of whatever material might have been handy at the moment.

As I gazed in stupefied wonder, I saw that a good portion of the structure was made of rock, though only some of that had been mortared. A second part was badly weathered adobe, and a third part was constructed of the same sort of rotting logs that had been used in the corrals. The fourth part was a small lean-to that looked to have been tacked onto the rest of the cabin at a more recent date, and it was constructed of faded tar paper nailed over whatever might have been underneath. The low roof was dirt, covered by the same dry weeds that grew everywhere else. And the whole pathetic assortment had been built up against a steep hillside, so that the entire back wall of the cabin was nothing more than hill.

But I wasn't really paying attention to such details at the time. Not only was I so hot and thirsty I felt like I could spit sand, but the unforgettable image of Mother's lifeless form was ever before me, filling me with a dark and bitter loathing for Carlos and the other cowards who had done it. I was fixed in my determination to get us away from this crazy Indian as soon as I could, and then to find a way to start getting even!

"When does it get dark?" I finally asked, thinking that would be the best time for JudyAnn and me to make our escape.

"Why, tonight, I be thinking." Gabriel Hurryup did not look back.

"Wasn't . . . it about sunset when you found us?"

The Indian looked back at me, his expression

inquisitive. Finally he laughed, that same shrill cackle that had so unnerved me an hour before. My favorite stories at the time were of witches and goblins and haunts and other such mysteries, and more and more I was thinking I had stumbled into something akin, and that I had been a fool to follow my parents' counsel.

"Sunset?" the man snorted as his strange laughter subsided. "No, laddie, it be morning now, and that were a sunrise ye awakened to. Ye and the wee thing in me arms must've slept the whole night through."

I was stunned. That meant it would soon be a full day since Mother had been killed, and whatever had happened to Father was now history. Unless, I thought with sudden dismay, JudyAnn and I had managed to sleep through *two* nights and a day—

"Miss Kizzy!" Gabriel Hurryup blurted as some chickens and a goat scattered before us. "Miss Kizzy, me bonnie lass, we be having guests for breakfast and maybe dinner, too. They haven't no possibles betwixt 'em, so break out the good stuff! Do ye hear?"

Seconds later the frail, dark-skinned woman Father had called Keziah Jane was standing before us on the stoop, wiping her hands on her apron as she looked to see who we were.

"Well, doo-da dah," she breathed as she stepped toward us, "if it don't be the Jones younguns! And traveling mighty light, too. This means that feller Jose Maria Carlos Louis Rivera Sebastian de Ortega Rejos has been about his work, Gabe darlin.' Don't ye think?"

"Aye, I'd say certain sure." Gabriel Hurryup's voice was quiet, calm. "But then, ye knew he would soon be up to something, didn't ye! Here ye go, Miss Kizzy. Take this precious wee thing before I drop her. Both she and young Cluvarious are in dire need of a drink, and then a little something else afterward."

All solicitous and concerned, Keziah Jane Hurryup took the still-sleeping JudyAnn from her husband's weakened arms, laid her over her own bony shoulder, and passed immediately back into the ramshackle cabin. And taking a long, deep breath to steady myself for I knew not what, I followed slowly after.

12

"There ye be, child," the woman said tenderly as she put JudyAnn down in a fine, soft chair. JudyAnn was just awakening, and so I took her hand so she wouldn't be too surprised by her new surroundings. Trouble was, there was no one there to help *me* get over *my* shock at the same thing, for the interior of that home was enough to shock anybody.

Whereas the outside of the Hurryup cabin had looked small, ramshackle, and decrepit, the inside was clean and tastefully decorated with things that could easily have come out of the very latest mail-order catalogues. It was also spacious, far larger than I would ever have imagined from the outside. It was much later before I finally realized that a good part of the home had been dug into the hillside rather than butted up against it as I had originally thought. The advantage of having a part of it underground, the constantly chattering Keziah Jane Hurryup explained to me, was that it remained either naturally warm or naturally cool, depending on the season.

All the inside walls were stuccoed and white-washed to a brightness that amazed me, and they were hung with fur pelts, a rifle, traps, and other amazing things. In the center of the room, but nearer the end that opened off into the tar-paper lean-to, was a funny-looking heating stove, while at the other end gaped a large, empty fireplace. Its emptiness didn't surprise me, though, for finding good logs for burning would have been a real problem in that barren country.

Two doors opened off the room toward the back; both were closed, so I could only speculate as to where they led. Several deeply padded, leather-covered chairs and sofas were placed about, and the smooth stone floor was scattered over with the deepest, thickest hides and carpets I had ever stepped on.

Mother's pride and joy had been her kitchen, and it seemed to be the same with Keziah Jane Hurryup. Her kitchen, located in the rear corner of the home to the left of the two doors, was apparently her kingdom, and there she ruled supreme. It was lined with cupboards filled with the most wonderful assortment of foodstuffs and other items. There were two long, stone counter-tops, a wondrously big iron stove that had two ovens below and a long warming oven up above the eight cooking plates, and a tall icebox that I later learned was cooled not with ice but with a steadily running stream of icy cold water. And it was that cold running water, which I was soon drinking with gusto despite its slightly acrid taste, that astounded me the most.

Mother had a pump in her kitchen that drew water directly out of our well, but it took her or Father or me a lot of effort to pump it up by hand. Mrs. Hurryup had instead a continually flowing stream that ran through a hollow log butting through the wall from somewhere in the hillside behind her kitchen. The log ended directly above her sink, which was made of hollowed-out stone, and there the water cascaded downward without ceasing, giving her all the water she could ever want or use. From a hole in the bottom of the sink it flowed on to somewhere else through a drain in her floor, meaning that the woman hardly ever had to haul dirty water out by the pail the way we had to do it at home.

"Where does all the water come from?" I finally asked the bustling Keziah Jane, my curiosity beating back my disdain. "And where does it go from here?"

"Well, doo-da dah if ye ain't the inquisitive one!" the woman declared, at the same time beaming at me as if I'd asked the most important questions in the world after she had coached me in each of them. And while her language was similar to Gabriel Hurryup's, Keziah Jane didn't form her words the same way her husband did. Neither did she roll her r's, and she used the word *ain't* all the time. No wonder Mother had thought of her as uncouth!

"The water comes from a wee spring that be inside the hill behind us," she responded brightly, "and be piped into me kitchen just as ye see. Hollowing this log were me sweet Gabe darlin's doings, it were, and these many years has it served me well."

"And after it empties through that hole in the floor?" I pressed.

Now the thin woman laughed, and I was uncomfortably aware of how much her laughter put me in mind of my mother. "Ah, Cluvarious, ye be a wonder, ye be! A-hating us and being curious about us, all to once? But that be a fine trait, lad. Never allow your prejudices to get in the way of your learning. So doo-da dah and on we go! It be into a cavity that the water flows, a monstrous natural cistern that carries it down off to goodness knows where."

"Cavity?" I questioned, my head spinning just with trying to understand her.

"Aye, an endless cavity in the rock. There be a horde of 'em along the edge of the Dome, fearful dark and deep, but I ain't been in ary but the one. For all I know, lad, they run all the way to China! Me sweet Gabe darlin,' though, he do poke around in 'em from time to time."

Endless cavities in the rock! I thought scornfully as I turned away, not for a second remembering Carlos's description of how faults, folds, and holes were formed along the edges of salt domes. Who did she think she was trying to snooker? Endless caves? Running all the way through the earth to China? Not only was Keziah Jane Hurryup an Indian, but she was also an idiot. Nobody had ever heard of caves in our part of the country! And to actually think that such a hole might run all the way through the earth?

It turned out that Mrs. Hurryup was an empty-headed chatterer when her husband was not around, going on and on about nothing much at all until I thought she would never stop. Of course, in JudyAnn she had probably met her match, for that girl could talk a blue streak any time she wanted, and when at play with her dolls she could carry on endless conversations between twenty or thirty of them at a time.

This last is probably a slight exaggeration, but I believe it makes my point. Keziah Jane Hurryup and my little sister seemed born for each other, and whenever Gabriel Hurryup disappeared, I might as well have not even existed. That was fine with me, for besides the fact that their chattering bored me silly, I wanted to look around—get the lay of the land, so to speak—and figure out how to effect our escape. Somehow I had to get the two of us out of there as quickly as I could, and I had to find out exactly what had happened to Father.

"Wagh," Gabriel Hurryup wheezed as he came through the heavy door a little later, having obviously been to somewhere and back in a big hurry, "Otis be on his way."

"Ye know?" Keziah Jane Hurryup questioned.

"Aye, he sent up a smoke." Turning to us, Gabriel

did his best to smile. "Well, me lad and wee bonnie lassie, has me sweet Miss Kizzy been chattering your ears off?" He cackled then, and his wife beamed like she'd just been paid the finest of compliments. "Ye'll be noticing that her teeth be new," he went on, grinning from ear to ear. "That'll be on account of she talks so much she wears out a set a year, and sometimes two. And why be she such a fast talker, says ye? Because, says I, her father were an auctioneer and her mother were a woman!"

Again the man's crazy cackling at his own humor peeled through the home. But he was right as rain about his wife, and I had to give him credit for that.

"Well, me wee lassie," Gabriel Hurryup continued, speaking now to my little sister, "be ye ready to eat?"

"Yes, thank you, sir," JudyAnn said politely as she slid from the chair and climbed onto a bench beside the heavy table. "I'm very hungry, and because Cluvarous always eats much more than me, I'll bet he's twice as hungry as I am!" Maybe I loved JudyAnn, but her obsequiousness with these miserable Indians sickened me, and for only the second or third time in my life I felt like popping her one, just to shut her up.

"Well, doo-da dah!" Mrs. Hurryup laughed delightedly as she placed platters of steaming food on the table: eggs, cold goat's milk, smoked side meat that I later learned was actually chicken, and something called grits that I wasn't very sure about but that JudyAnn absolutely relished.

Gabriel Hurryup said a strange sort of grace, and after that we all piled into what I was forced to admit was some of the best-tasting food I had ever eaten. In fact, I couldn't seem to get my fill.

"Well, doo-da dah, lad!" Mrs. Hurryup exclaimed happily after my fourth or fifth helping of food. "Ye be eating like ye have a tapeworm!"

"Or two of 'em," Gabriel agreed as he pushed his own plate away. "But that do bring up a point, me sweet Miss Kizzy. If a feller like young Cluvarious here can get silk from a silkworm, why can't he get tape from a tapeworm?"

Again the crazy old man's cackle rang out, joined by his silly wife's giggle, and now I was really starting to wonder what sort of mess we had gotten ourselves into. In fact, after things had been washed up with hot water drawn from one of the big stove's two reservoirs, I went back to carefully examining all the stuff in that huge room, trying to figure out a way of using it to get away.

"Did you kill all these animals?" I asked Gabriel Hurryup skeptically as I moved along one wall, gently touching one furry skin and then another.

The man had seated himself in what I was to discover was his favorite chair, his still-moccasined feet stretched out on a stuffed ottoman. "Aye, lad," he responded with a nod, "this child trapped a heap, and boatloads more besides."

Gabriel had taken off his hat before eating but had instantly replaced it with another—a soft felt beret set at a steep angle on his head. The shiny half-dome that was exposed, however, led me to believe that the man was hairless. After another furtive glance, I was just as astounded to discover that he did not even have eyebrows and eyelashes. Apparently Gabriel Hurryup was bald as a billiard ball—a very un-Indian-like trait, I had to admit—and wore his hats indoors and out to hide the shame of it. The very thought of such vanity filled me with scorn, and I couldn't seem to stop myself from letting him know how I felt.

"How long have you been hairless?" I questioned disdainfully.

"Only since I lost it all," he cackled by way of reply. "I were thinking once of getting meself a toupee to cover things up, but me sweet Miss

Kizzy, she thought it would be like putting a new top on a wagon what had worn out its wheels!" Again his unnerving laughter filled the room. "Nachural, laddie, me being bald don't matter to me sweet Miss Kizzy. Not at all! Why, the onliest time she ever calls me handsome be when this ol' hoss opens me possibles to check me coin and she says, 'Handsome over!'" Now the old fool was cackling so hard he was slapping his leg, and I was feeling sorry I had brought the subject up.

"'Twere once a fine land for taking plews," he continued, his laughter abruptly gone and his look somehow far away and not upon me at all. "Wild and free as the wind, lad, with nothing but miles and miles of country spread out betwixt more miles and miles of the same. But things always change, they do, and the country be wild no more, nor free, either one. Change has done for the beaver and the elk and the bear, and she'll soon be doing for the deer and the wolf and the painter. Aye, and maybeso every other decent critter the good Lord ever formed."

"A painter? I haven't ever heard of—"

"It be a monstrous cat, laddie, a mountain lion, with eyes of fire and jaws of steel and a yowl at night that'll break a man's heart it sounds so like the cry of a bad-wounded woman or a baby in distress. That be a painter!"

"Humph! Well, I don't see how you can call mountain lions decent critters, or wolves either!" I was responding haughtily, thinking as I did of an adventure story that I had once read about ravenous, attacking wolves. But no matter how much venom I put into my voice, the man would not be baited.

"Aye, lad," he responded quietly, "there be many who might agree with ye, though I won't be amongst 'em, especially not where wolves be concerned. Why, says ye? Because, says I, the wolf's near human in his thinking, and I won't be caught naysaying against him."

"Human?" By now I was almost mocking him. "How could a wolf ever be thought of as human?"

"How, indeed?" the Indian responded as his eyes closed and he seemed to sink into his chair. "Well, ol' hoss, I'll tell ye, and then ye'll be leaving me alone in me diggings for a spell so's I can take me snooze. Hear ye?"

"I hear," I growled sullenly.

"Well," he began, his eyes still closed, "it were back in the winter of ought five or ought six, most of a hundred year ago now, in a wee valley on the upper Missouri near where the Yellerstone cuts in. The snow were five foot deep on the level and it were cold, too, so cold the words froze in a feller's mouth and popped out silent, not making a sound until they hit the ground and shattered.

"'Course this child were a lone man in the wilderness that winter, so frozen words made no matter. What did were the awful terrible cold and the fact that I had me burning a mighty big fire so's I wouldn't cache in me plews before morning."

"What's a plew?" I asked without thinking, somehow as caught up in his strange tale as I had always been in Mother's stories.

"Beaver plew, lad. Fur! Skin! Pelt! It's them what lines the wall yonder, and it were what this child were after one year to the next when I were a trapper and a trader. Why, says ye? Because, says I, it were the only thing that put the coin in me possibles. Do ye get me drift?"

I nodded, though I'm not at all certain he opened his eyes to see me.

"Wagh!" he continued, "there this child were, all alone and doing me best to get a wee bit of shut-eye before the fire burned low. But the cold reached in and chilled me bones anyhow, so I rolled towards the fire to warm me other side, and that were when

I seed I were no longer alone. No sir, this ol' hoss had been joined across the fire by a big gray wolf, who were squatted on his haunches with his eyes closed and his head nodding with drowsiness most as much as mine had been a wee bit afore!"

"But . . . weren't you scared?" I asked as I pictured the wild, ragged wolf in my mind. Afterward, when I realized how easily I had allowed myself to get caught up in Gabriel Hurryup's tale, I was plenty disgusted with myself.

"Aye, laddie, for certain. But being skeered's all right. Backin' away ain't. Any time this ol' hoss'd start shiverin' with fear he'd say, 'Gabe, ye knuckle-headed idjit, ye got yourself into this fix, and so what comes ye can just take!' And after that me fear weren't so terrible bad.

"But to get on with it, this son had seen wolves come close to the fire before, mind ye, but only to steal scraps of meat. Never in all me born days had I seen one come up solely to warm hisself! That were human doings, I tell ye, human doings! And I saw it plain.

"Well, this old fool watched that wolf for a spell, saw that he was basking in the heat as much if not more'n me, and so I rolled over and went back to sleep, leaving him to the quiet enjoyment of the flames. Nachural he was gone come morning, but since then I've heard tell of wolves pulling wee children from burning barns and the like, and raising them as their own. Having seen what I did that night by my fire, I'm inclined to believe it. That's why I tell ye, laddie, that a wolf be more human critter than otherwise."

And once again, "Humph!" was the only thing I could think of to say.

13

"Clue, why don't you like the Hurryups? Father sent us here, if you'll remember, and they've shown us nothing but kindness."

It was late. Through the day I had explored as much as I could both inside and out, and now JudyAnn and I had been put to bed in the low-roofed lean-to. Or rather, JudyAnn had been put to bed. I had gone on my own a little later, and was still dressed and lying on top of the blankets, waiting for the right moment to take my sister and make our break. The room, finely finished just like the rest of the strange house, held two small beds, which caused me to wonder if perhaps the Hurryups might indeed have had children in the long ago. But whereas JudyAnn's room at home was filled with dolls and other nonsense, and mine held such treasures as a wagon, two spinning tops, half a dozen willow fishing poles, and loads of marbles and other important items, this room held nothing—nothing but the two beds and an empty chest. If the Hurryups had had children, I concluded, they certainly hadn't been much on collecting mementos.

"JudyAnn," I finally growled, "these fool Indians are the cause of Mother and maybe even Father getting killed! Can't you see that? There's no way I'm ever going to like them! And there's no way I'm going to stay here, either!"

"I don't think they're Indians, Clue. They don't even talk like Indians. Why, except for saying dooda dah all the time, Miss Kizzy talks just like So-Help-Me Hannah!"

"As if that's a great recommendation," I snorted. "Besides, you ever been around any real Indians?"

"No, but I'll bet a whole two bits you haven't either."

"You don't have two bits to bet."

"Maybe not, but if I did, I'd bet it! And you'd lose, too. I know, because I heard you tell Skipper that the Hurryups are the only real Indians you've ever met. So there!"

It was too dark to see, but I knew JudyAnn was sticking out her tongue at me. It angered me, too—

not her tongue so much as her being right. I had told Skipper that very thing, right after meeting the Hurryups.

"You know, Jude, I've seen plenty of pictures of Indians, and folks in the Thespian's Club are always dressing up like them for their performances. The Chautauqua Club is always doing readings about them, too. So it isn't that I'm completely ignorant concerning what Indians look like."

"Neither am I, Cluvarous Jones!"

"Then you should know that the Hurryups look like Indians! And what about the awful way they talk? It's clear they weren't brought up to speak English like normal folk!"

I grinned into the darkness, knowing that this last evidence had finally gotten to her. Mother had taught us to despise bad grammar. The Hurryups were filled with it, and that was why she was not responding.

"Jude," I said then, trying my best to sound friendly again, "I don't want to argue with you, not now. We've got to stick together until we can get out of here and back to town."

JudyAnn was silent. "Clue," she finally said, changing the subject altogether, "do you miss Mother?"

"'Course I do," I responded, determined to be strong but nevertheless feeling the rush of tears swelling behind my eyes.

"Me too. . . . Do you think she's really dead?"

I swallowed hard before answering. "I think she is, JudyAnn. She certainly looked dead."

"I thought so too. But she talked to me, Clue, and so I don't know—"

"She talked to you?" I questioned as I rose onto my elbow. This seemed eerie, especially because I was so certain that Mother had also spoken with me. "What'd she say?"

"Well, partly she told me to stay with you, and to help you remember your manners."

"My manners?" I questioned, so upset that I didn't think about asking what else JudyAnn might have been told. "My manners are just dandy!"

"Not when you say bad things about the Hurryups, they aren't. Remember, Cluvarous, if it weren't for their being so nice to us, we'd be alone and lost somewhere in those awful hills!"

"So was Carlos nice," I sneered, "at first! Offering me cookies and telling things so I'd understand them. And he turned out to be a murderer, Jude, starting up the lynch-mob that killed Mother and maybe even Father!"

"Yes, I suppose that's true." JudyAnn sighed. "But Clue, I . . . I'm scared . . . I'm scared about Mother."

"You mean you're lonely?"

Again JudyAnn sighed, and I had the feeling then that she was crying, but trying to do it quietly so I wouldn't know. "I'm very lonely," she finally replied, "and I . . . I'm having a hard time remembering what Mother looked like."

I was surprised, for that was a problem I hadn't even thought of, but it instantly became worrisome. "Just close your eyes, Jude." I was forcing myself to sound positive, hoping my suggestion would work for both of us. "Then you can see her fine."

"Uh-uh," she argued softly, "I've tried it, and I can't. What I see is her laying in that darn old road with that welt and blood on her face. That's all I can see, Clue. Dirt and blood! What . . . what if I can't remember her in a pretty way, ever again?"

"Well," I replied, searching desperately for an answer that we would both find comforting, "I suppose you could look in a mirror, Jude. What with your olive complexion, dark eyes, and dark hair, Father is always saying how you put him in mind of her. And just the other day I heard So-Help-Me

Hannah telling Mother that sometimes you acted more like Mother, even, than Mother herself."

"Did she really say that? Honest?"

"I swear on the bones of old Captain Kidd the Pirate!"

JudyAnn giggled. "As if you had any of Captain Kidd's bones to swear on."

"I'd swear on them if I did!"

"Clue?"

"Yeah?"

"Do *you* think I look like Mother?"

Rolling onto my back, I stared up at the ceiling. "Actually, Jude, I'm starting to see it more and more." I was, too, especially in the way she had of turning up her face at a little angle, smiling, and speaking with folks in such a fine, polite way. Mother had done it the same. And that resemblance quite naturally made me wonder if I might ever be tall and handsome like Father. It wasn't likely, I admitted, but deep down I was hoping.

"We'll give things a little longer to quiet down," I said then, speaking softly into the darkness. "Then you can get dressed and we'll get out of here."

"We'll be disobeying Father, Clue. Mother too."

"No we won't, Jude. They told us to come here, and we did. But they didn't know that the

Hurryups had fooled Father and helped cause all our troubles, and we do. That's why we have to get away. We've got to let folks know the truth—that us townfolks deserve that money Carlos has been bragging on, every nickel."

"And find Father?"

"Of course! And find Father."

"But . . . what if we're wrong? About the Hurryups and their money, I mean."

"We aren't wrong! Remember, I'm older than you, so I know things you can't be expected to know. You've heard Mother say that very thing a bunch of times, so it's got to be true." Mother *had* said it, but only in pointing out to me, always in moments of chastisement, that it was unfair of me to expect eleven-going-on-twelve-year-old male thinking and behavior from a barely nine-year-old girl. So I was twisting Mother's words terribly, hoping my sister wouldn't notice.

And there was something else nagging at me, something I didn't even want to think about, let alone discuss with JudyAnn. In my explorations that day I had come onto a very old book, bound in leather. I wasn't certain what it was, because it had been printed in a language that meant nothing to me. In the front of the book, however, were three pages of handwritten lists that were also unintelligible, except, that is, for some numbers that might have denoted long-past years. But again I wasn't sure, and so I was quite ready to tell myself that it couldn't have been the Bible Father had spoken of, the one that had verified for him Gabriel Hurryup's Gaelic ancestry.

"Oh, very well," JudyAnn sighed with resignation. "I'll go. But I still don't think the Hurryups are real Indians."

"And I know better," I growled unhappily as I swung my feet off the bed and onto the floor. "Now, get up and get dressed, Jude, and do it quiet! The sooner I can get us out of this place, the happier I'm going to be!"

14

"Why, laddie, are ye fixing to leave us without so much as a proper adieu?"

JudyAnn and I were out in the large room, creeping silently toward the door, when Gabriel Hurryup's voice rasped out of the darkness, stopping us in our tracks. Quickly I pushed my sister down behind a chair while I ducked down beside her, hoping against hope that utter silence might convince the strange man, wherever he was, that he had not heard us at all.

"Aye, lad," he said then, with a sound of laughter in his voice, "ye be passing quiet, I allow, but not near so quiet as the Rickaree. They snuck in on this child once, but that were the only and last time. And even so I put 'em under, ever man-jack one o' them red sons but the one, and he were singing songs about me for years afterward. Wagh!"

JudyAnn started to rise; I grabbed her arm and pulled her back down. A match flared, and suddenly the room was bathed with lantern light.

"There! Now get ye up from behind that chair, ye and the wee lassie both, and come and sit by the fire. I be thinking it be time we made a bit of medicine together. *Get up, I say!*"

Having no idea what medicine the crazy Indian was talking about, and sensing that I had somehow raised his hackles, I nudged my sister, and together we rose to our feet.

"You sure did wake up grouchy," I muttered as I followed JudyAnn toward where the old man was seated.

"Did not!" Gabriel Hurryup snorted. "Actual, lad, I always do my best to let her sleep!"

With that sorry humor he broke into his crazy, cackling laughter, and with a glance at each other just to reassure ourselves, JudyAnn and I took seats on one of his huge couches.

"Tell the truth, lad, I never judge me sweet Miss Kizzy for her shortcomings. If it weren't for them, I'd never have got her in the first place!" Again his crazy laughter peeled forth. "Fact is, the first time I asked her she turned me down flat, only allowing that she did admire me good taste." Now old

Gabriel Hurryup was gasping for air he was laughing so hard, and JudyAnn and I could do nothing but stare. "When Miss Kizzy and me finally tied the knot, though, it were for better or for worse. Thing is, I got the better and she got the worse! 'Course she counters that by saying that marriages be made in heaven, after which this ol' hoss has to remind her that so be thunder and lightning!"

Well, the old man was cackling so hard at his own awful jokes, slapping his leg and rocking back and forth at the same time, that I didn't know if he was ever going to recover. JudyAnn squeezed my hand just to get a grip on something normal, I suppose, and I was squeezing back pretty hard myself, looking around at anything else but him. And that was when I finally noticed that it was no lantern that was lighting the room, but the fireplace. And it was blazing merrily despite that I could see no sign of firewood. Suddenly I realized that neither had I seen any firewood in the kitchen, though of course Mrs. Hurryup had done a lot of cooking on her huge stove.

"Where's the wood?" I asked in awe, hoping that the crazy old Indian was still sane enough to answer.

"Why, laddie," he gasped, doing his best to take

control of himself, "where, indeed? That be an oil fireplace ye see before ye—a stone basin filled with burning oil."

"Oil?" I replied, thunderstruck. "So, Carlos was right?"

"Well, in a manner of speaking, I reckon so."

"And oil heats Mrs. Hurryup's kitchen stove?"

Gabriel Hurryup, now very sober, turned his head and pointed with his chin. "Aye, and the one behind ye too. There be a bit of oil here on the place, enough for us and I suppose a wee bit more besides, but nowhere near what friend Carlos be leading them sorry townsfolk to believe."

"But . . . but how do you know? He's a geologist, and—"

"Laddie, there be other geologists than Carlos de Ortega. We brung a dozen onto the place ten, twelve year back. I invited 'em from here and yonder, thinking maybe we had something lots of folks could use. They even sunk a few holes, but I had 'em do it in places where the townsfolk wouldn't see. That were on account of I didn't want to stir up no hornet's nest when there weren't no need. Turned out I were right, too. Every hole came up dry."

"Dry?"

"Aye, dry as a year-old Rickaree scalp. No oil, not one drop, not anywhere around this entire dome of salt we be setting to the side of. Why, says ye? Because, says I, there weren't no decent caprock put there by the good Lord to hold the oil down. So she's escaped, them geologist fellers told me, most of it so long ago there aren't but the faintest sign of it left. What is, and it be only a tiny seep in the cave behind the house here that I've walled off into a well to give it a bit of a drop, Miss Kizzy and me make use of as we can."

Stunned, I could hardly keep my head from spinning. "But . . . but Carlos, he told us that—"

"I reckon I can guess what Carlos told ye," Gabriel Hurryup interrupted, "and I say the man's a fool and should've had his topknot lifted right after he was given all them fancy names. Would've saved us all a heap of trouble, it would have, and kept your ma's life intact in the bargain. I told him the whole tale, even showed him what I could of the dry holes, though not the seep in the cave, which I reckon is best kept secret from folks like him. It never made no matter, though, for he insisted on giving the Dome country another try. I turned him down flat. He offered to buy the place with his company's money, and I turned him down even flatter. That were when he threatened to put Miss Kizzy and me under the sod and drill his fool holes anyhow.

"That were also when I hauled old Betsy off'n the wall there and ordered him to skedaddle." Gabriel Hurryup suddenly cackled again. "Thing were, laddie, old Betsy ain't held a powder-charge in forty year, and ain't carried a flint in that long, neither. She's plumb wore out! I'd of had to club the man to death if'n I'd really meant to kill him. He didn't know that, though, and you should've seen him tuck his tail and run." And again Gabriel Hurryup burst into his strange and unsettling cackle.

Well, I was stumped. I didn't know what to think, or do, or say. There was oil but there wasn't. Carlos had threatened to kill the Hurryups because they wouldn't let him drill or sell him their place, just like he had threatened my parents when Father wouldn't agree to issue a new deed, and—

"Wait a minute!" I growled, my mind suddenly clear again. "You said Carlos offered to buy your place, but I say you're lying. He wouldn't have done that, not when he knew you were Indian. It's against the law in this country for Indians to own land!"

Again Gabriel Hurryup cackled. "Aye, laddie," he

finally said when his crazy merriment had passed, "I heard ye augering with the wee lass there afore ye tried sneaking out, telling her how wise and smart ye were. Well, ye aren't, for she were right as fresh rain and ye be wrong as a putrefactin' elk in a stale buffalo waller. If I were Injun I'd be proud to own up to it, ye can allow to that! But I ain't, and neither be Miss Kizzy!"

"I don't believe you," I snapped angrily. "You dress and walk like an Indian, you talk strange, your skin's dark, and you don't shave—"

"Laddie, I don't hardly know whether to sorrow more for ye or for that wee little lassie a-setting there beside ye, for she comes near to worshipping ye. Of a truth ye remind me of the old feller what allowed that if he'd knowed he was going to live so long, he'd have taken better care of his health. Or if Lady Godiva had ridden sidesaddle down the streets of Coventry, only half the folks would've had reason to cheer. Ye be looking at things all crooked, lad, and couldn't see the plain truth if it marched up and whacked ye on the noggin. I tell ye, that sort of thinking'll get ye put under sure, and maybe the wee lassie with ye!"

"And we're supposed to just believe you?" I was still angry, which is why I was speaking so rudely to Gabriel Hurryup. Normally I would never have spoken to an adult that way; I wouldn't have dared, but besides that, I'd also been taught better by both my parents. And I would also have acknowledged JudyAnn's pointed nudges in my side, which I totally ignored. But on account of all that had transpired in the previous few days, I don't think I was really being myself. The amazing thing, then and now, is that Gabriel Hurryup still didn't rise up and put me in my place. He just sat there quietly, his hands folded together and his eyes trained on me.

"Lad," he said calmly, "this child knew a Mandan brave once who were tolerable like ye. He wouldn't believe a thing unless he were shown, and then on occasion he wouldn't believe it anyhow. Finally a French trapper who carried the name Pierre Pambrun took a long knife and showed the Mandan his own insides. Split him open wide. That ended the Mandan's doubts for good."

So saying, Gabriel Hurryup slowly unbuttoned his shirt cuffs and rolled up his sleeves, revealing skinny arms so white they reminded me of the underbelly of a dead fish.

"Are ye satisfied?" he asked with eyes flashing.

Slowly I nodded.

He cackled briefly. "This child thought ye might

be. A hundred and twenty-something year of sun and wind'll do that to a man's skin, and turn it to old leather besides—"

"A hundred and twenty years!" I exclaimed, knowing in the instant that I had absolutely caught him in his lies. Nobody lived a hundred and twenty-something years! Nobody! Especially not and still gallivant around the country faster than a turpentined cat and look young enough to be Father's age or maybe even younger. In fact, the only thing about Gabriel Hurryup that looked old was his baldness and the dewlap of skin hanging under his chin. So what if he did have white skin under his shirt! He could easily have done something to it that would be good enough to fool a kid like me, especially in the light of that oil fire! And as for his crazy claims—

"Now I know you're lying!" I almost shouted. "I know what old folks look and act like, and I'm talking fifty, sixty, sometimes maybe even seventy years. You don't look or act it either one, and there's no way on this earth you're going to tell me you're a hundred and twenty years old!"

For what seemed a long time Gabriel Hurryup merely looked at me. "Well, lad," he finally said, sounding tired, "ye be right. I'm not a hundred and twenty years old, at least not exact. If it be the truth ye want, the whole truth, and if this be the year nineteen and ought four, then actually this child be nearer a hundred and twenty-seven. Truth be told, though, I don't much keep track of it the way I used to."

"But . . . but that's not possible! Nobody can live that long!"

"Yes they can, Clue." JudyAnn was speaking quietly, her voice filled with pleading. "Mother told me about a Bible man who was named Methu . . . Methu—"

"Methuselah," I growled, feeling unaccountably upset at JudyAnn's memory.

"Yes, Methuselah! Mother told me he was more than nine hundred years old, and that's tons more than a hundred and twenty-seven."

"Yeah, and Methuselah was one of God's miracles!" I countered.

"How do you know Gabriel isn't a miracle too?"

"A miracle!" I snorted disdainfully.

"Aye, laddie," Gabriel grinned, not cackling but looking like he was going to start up at any instant, "miracle or not, me age be a great mystery, don't it. Others, better men than ye, have thought the same. Though truth be known, it be nowhere near as great a mystery as why ye won't believe I aren't Injun. That be a mystery that'd perplex ol' Solomon hisself! Howsomever, in case doubts are still finding entertainment in that hollow space betwixt your ears, I'll show ye a wee bit more."

Slowly Gabriel Hurryup lifted his hand, took hold of his beret, and with a flourish swept it off and bent forward so I could better see the crown of his head.

And then I was stumped but good. High on the crown of his head, but off to the side so it had been hidden under his beret, was a circle of pure white maybe two inches across. It was surrounded by skin that was almost as white, but puckered around the edges so I could plainly discern that the white in the center of the circle was bone.

"Do ye see, laddie?" he was asking as I stared. "Do ye see where that one Rickaree brave lifted me topknot that terrible night? Left me for dead, too, he did. But this child were too ornery to cache in me plews, besides which Miss Kizzy were a-waiting for me in St. Louis, and I couldn't let her down."

"You . . . you were scalped?" I gulped while JudyAnn cried out and buried her face against my arm so she wouldn't have to look. "By an Indian?"

"Aye," Gabriel Hurryup replied as he reached up

and began softly massaging around the ancient wound, "by that same Rickaree brave I been telling ye of. Me topknot were lifted by that lucky son, sure as ol' Betsy there used to shoot, which is why I know he sung songs about me. That were their way, ye know—singing about the bravery of the folks they'd killed so as to make their own deeds look better."

"When did it . . . happen?" I was trying to get my mind in gear again, but the sight of that bare patch of skull was so overwhelming that it was all I could do just to talk. I had no idea people could live through being scalped! In fact, at the moment I seemed to have no ideas at all!

"Wagh, lad," he responded to my question, stopping his massage to stroke his chin thoughtfully, "I don't hardly know the day, not exactly. But I've always calculated it to be about the fifteenth of March in the year ought eight."

"Ought eight?"

"Aye, eighteen hundred and ought eight. The middle of March, as I recollect."

The old man carefully placed his beret back over the ancient wound on his head and settled it in place. Then, just as carefully, he adjusted his position in the soft leather chair and readjusted his feet on the ottoman.

Gabriel's Well

"It were July before I finally dragged meself back down to St. Louis," he continued, "and it were in August when me and Miss Kizzy—" Suddenly he grinned, almost as if he were embarrassed. "Miss Kizzy were what I were calling the little woman even then, lad. Her true and maiden name were Keziah Jane Murphy, but I couldn't ever seem to get past calling her Miss Kizzy, same as her calling me Gabe darlin' instead of a proper Gabriel. So in August of ought eight, once I were home to St. Louis and feeling well as might be expected considering I had lost me topknot, she and me had a preacher tie the knot and marry us up proper. That's how come I remember it so well."

"So you've been married . . . ninety-six years?" To be honest, I could not even comprehend such a claim.

"Aye, if this be the year nineteen hundred and ought four, which your father swore it were the last time Miss Kizzy and me were at the bank."

Slowly I shook my head, trying to clear my mind. "What . . . what's a Rickaree?" I asked then, looking for a safer path to tread.

"Law, laddie, don't ye know a single blessed thing? A Rickaree's an Injun. *Arikara* be the proper way of saying it, though most I knew say it same as me. Name means 'men with horns,' which is how the bones they wore in their hair made 'em look. They were a branch of the devil Pawnee, but every bit as mean, a real scourge along the upper Missouri during the first years of the last century. More'n one of us free trappers fell to their treacherous ways, I tell ye!"

"You really were a trapper?"

Gabriel Hurryup's eyes twinkled. "Aye, lad," he said as he reached up and readjusted the soft beret. "A trapper and a trader and a curly old he-wolf, for certain. Can't sleep no more on account of it, neither. Besides that me missing topknot pains me fierce when I'm down and abed, every time I close my eyes I see that grinning Rickaree with his knife a-whackin' at my scalp; him or more'n a hundred other fine braves what I fought and maybeso killed whilst I were peeling plews and traipsing about them far-off, high-up hills. They're always painted for war and attacking me, them Injuns I can see in my head, screeching and yelling worse'n a whole flock of magpies. Such doings aren't much help for sleeping, I tell ye.

"Lassie," he said then, for the first time addressing JudyAnn directly, "if ye've a mind to go back to bed, have at 'er. The lad and me have a wee bit of palavering to do before the sun creeps up across them eastern hills."

Without a word JudyAnn stood up and gave me a good-night peck on the cheek, which I normally wouldn't have allowed but which that night seemed just fine.

"Remember to mind your manners, Cluvarous," she said sweetly. "Mother told me to tell you."

"I will," I grumbled in return, not really even feeling bad at her reminder.

Flashing me a smile, JudyAnn then went over and kissed a beaming Gabriel Hurryup, and without another word to either of us she turned and walked back into the lean-to bedroom we had so confidently crept out of nearly an hour before.

And me? Well, I sat back in that glove-soft leather couch while the light from the oil-fed fire danced about the room, casting weird shadows that, under Gabriel Hurryup's almost magic spell, began looking for all the world like Indians and bears and wolves. Then for the rest of that night I listened to the most astounding assemblage of stories—tall tales or otherwise—that I had ever heard or ever expect to hear.

15

"Where's old Gab . . . I mean, Mr. Hurryup?" I grumbled as I stumbled out of our lean-to bedroom the next morning. JudyAnn might have had plenty of sleep and so was all bright-eyed and bushy-tailed, but for most of the night I'd had my ears talked off by the crazy old mountain man, and felt grumpy, as my father used to put it, as an old bear. "He said we were going traipsing this morning!"

Keziah Jane Hurryup, busy in her kitchen, laughed as though I'd said the funniest thing in the world. "Well, doo-da dah, lad! I do believe ye've taken a liking to me Gabe darlin'."

"He told Clue lots of exciting stories last night," JudyAnn tossed in helpfully, earning a well-deserved scowl from her older brother, "after he caught us trying to sneak out and escape."

Again the strange woman cackled. "So, ye had

yourselves a hankering for another try at the great outdoors, did ye? Well, lad, that ain't altogether bad, not according to me darlin' Gabe. He says it be nachural for a man to be fiddle-footed and on the move." She laughed again. "I say, though, that it were only his excuse to get out of doing woman things about the home place, which me Gabe darlin' avoided like the plagues of Egypt. But come on, the both of ye, and let's be off to relieve Jezebel of her udder of milk."

"Is Jezebel the name of your goat?" JudyAnn asked brightly as we followed the bucket-carrying Keziah Jane out the door.

"Aye, child, and she be the most cantankerous nanny this side of the Rocky Mountains. Oh, and to answer your question, lad, me Gabe darlin' be off to palaver with friend Otis, if he be about. Don't ye be fearin', though, for ye'll get your traipsing in soon enough, I gainsay."

"You mean there're other fool Indians in these hills?"

"I don't know about Injuns, but friend Otis usually be about."

With that the old lady charged through the corral, scattering squawking chickens everywhere, and headed down a trail that skirted the upthrust that was the Dome. JudyAnn ran and skipped to keep up, chattering constantly; though still in a sour mood, I kicked rocks along the trail behind. Not only had I not enjoyed much sleep but I was hungry, and I thought we should have been served a little breakfast before setting out to milk the fool goat.

"Is Gabe—I mean, Mr. Hurryup—really from Scotland?" I asked a little later when Keziah Jane was squatted behind the tethered nanny.

"Aye, lad," she said as she sent streams of warm milk into her pail. "Me Gabe darlin' were born of a goodly woman and a harsh old man in County Ross of the Scottish Highlands, back in the year of seventeen hundred and seventy-seven. Trouble were, at the time there were terrible animosity between the great Scottish clans, and it grew worse as he came of age and began to cast his eyes upon the bonnie lasses. When true love struck, me poor darlin' had the misfortune of falling for the lovely daughter of a rival clan leader."

"Why was that a misfortune?" Since JudyAnn had not heard the old trapper carrying on the night before, she was asking questions that I thought were a bother.

"Why? Because their intentions were to marry,

child." Keziah Jane stopped working the goat for a moment and looked up, her eyes blazing. "But in a fit of anger, the harsh man who had sired him took the very life from my darlin' Gabe's sweet lassie."

"He didn't kill her!" I insisted, horrified at the thought.

"But he did, lad," Keziah Jane breathed, her visage bleak, "with his own saber."

Dropping her face, the old woman set to work on Jezebel again. "After that, it were as though all the demons of hell were loosed upon the clans, and bloody was the war that followed. Not willing to slay the family of his true love, and not able to slay his own father despite that I think he needed it, me Gabe darlin' gathered his possibles and left in the dark of a bloody night. And with him, lad, to punish his father as best he could, me darlin' took the grandest treasure of them all—the true and only record and proof of his father's ancestry, and as well of his own. With him, lad, he fetched his father's Holy Bible!"

At this news I squirmed uncomfortably, though I said nothing. But not seeming to notice, Keziah Jane continued, telling us that Gabriel Hurryup had then fled to America, or so the story went, vowing as he stepped ashore in New York that he would never again speak or be known by the despised name of his father. By 1802 he had changed his name, moved west, and settled in St. Clair County, Illinois. It was there, nearly five years later, that he had met Keziah Jane Murphy, an orphan girl serving as an indentured servant to a wealthy family in Cahokia, across the Mississippi from St. Louis.

"You were really an indentured servant?" JudyAnn questioned.

"Aye, lass, I were. Me folks were struck with cholera, or black-leg as we called it. They died, and all nine of me brothers and sisters followed, one after the other. I were about your brother's age at the time, and in spite of caring for them all, I never once took ill."

"What did you do? I mean, after they had all died." In spite of myself, I was as curious about Mrs. Hurryup's tales as I had been about her husband's.

"Why, I saw to their burials. Then I burnt the cabin to kill the disease, sold the ground for a twenty-dollar gold piece, and paid it all for passage on a flatboat to St. Louis. Having nothing but one old dress of me mother's and a few papers, I signed a contract of indenture with some fine folks in

Cahokia. I done me work as I had promised, they raised me up proper, and they never charged me a cent for anything."

"Did they pay you?"

Keziah Jane cackled. "Lawsy, no! That weren't the way of things, lad. But when I married me darlin' Gabe in the year eighteen hundred and ought eight, after me contract of indenture had been fulfilled, the folks give me a fine dowry—three bolts of cloth, two bags of flour, a cooking kettle, me four favorite knickknacks, and three twenty-dollar gold pieces, which were a fortune in them days. With some of the money, me darlin' Gabe bought a fine little house in nearby Turkey Hill, on what later became known as American Bottom. It were there that we settled down."

With some difficulty she stripped the last of Jezebel's milk from her udder, pulled the nearly full pail away, and rose to her feet.

"Over the next thirty year we had an even dozen younguns—eight boys and four sweet lassies. They were wondrous children, too, and more lovely and beautiful than a mother can say."

"Where are they now?" JudyAnn asked innocently, before I could stop her.

"They be with the good Lord, child." Keziah Jane

smiled, and then bit her lip. "Well, doo-da dah," she breathed in embarrassment, "and after all these years!" She then swiped at her eyes with the sleeve of her dress.

"They all died?" My sister sounded astounded, and I could no more imagine it than she.

"Aye, child." Already the frail woman was controlling her emotions and reassuming her usual happy face. "Me first were killed in a wagon accident, me next two drowned in that terrible river what used to take me darlin' Gabe away, me fourth were shot by an evil man on account of he wouldn't leave off of riverboat gambling, and the rest died like me own family—of two separate but terrible plagues."

"Two?"

"Aye, two! The first were black-leg, which I had seen before and so saved one from certain death. But then, not many years later, we all come down with something they called diphtheria, and that time I were the only one who didn't pass on. Even me wee new babe died in me arms, and that whilst I were praying and pleading for the good Lord to spare her life and let her live."

"That . . . must have been awful!"

"It were, child. And it be tragic still, for it has left

us childless in our old ages, and so the pain of it never quite goes away. But the good Lord giveth, and the good Lord taketh away. Blessed be the name of the Lord."

We stood there for a moment, everything still except for the nanny Jezebel, who was now chewing contentedly on a nearby clump of dried weeds. There was no doubt I felt uncomfortable, for Miss Kizzy's stories were as outlandish as her husband's had been and just as unthinkable. And yet, though I doubted her, in that stillness I had the absolute conviction that her dozen children had indeed been lost. I could almost see them, feel them around me.

Abruptly then my thoughts turned to Mother and Father, and, not able to handle the sudden pain, I turned and fled for the house.

16

For the next two days, while JudyAnn and Mrs. Hurryup were chattering and doing what they called woman things around and about the home place, Gabriel Hurryup and I were always together. He had me exploring the Dome and everywhere else nearby, and he was pacing along beside me all the while, pointing out things he thought I might be interested in seeing. And all along I was doing my level best to figure out if the self-proclaimed trapper and mountain man was honest but crazy, or if he was the grandest liar I had ever known, which seemed more likely.

After dark each night we sat together around the oil-fed fireplace and listened while Gabriel read out of his old Bible—for so his book had turned out to be—rendering strange and sometimes incomprehensible translations of the ancient Gaelic language. It was a solemn time for JudyAnn and me, and listening to Gabriel while the flickering light threw dancing shadows on the walls and ceiling around us made it even more so.

During the daylight hours, though, the strange man showed me the decade-old dry wells, now capped, and explained why the geologists had drilled where they had. He showed me what was left of the dugout where the original rancher had lived back in the 1850s while he ranched the greener land southwest of the Dome. In a deep arroyo he also showed me the huge, powder-dry piles of bones where thousands of the rancher's cattle had been wiped out by a single winter's blizzard, bringing about his willingness to sell out to Gabriel and Keziah Jane Hurryup the following spring.

He showed me the huge circumference of the Dome, and told me that long before the time of the white man, Indians had thought of it as a sacred place. On top of the hill, maybe a quarter to half a mile behind the Hurryup place, he showed me a hole down into some rocks, about the size of a badger hole or a little larger, that was surrounded with old Indian arrow points made of stone, all pointed inward. In response to my questions, he explained that the Indians had considered the hole to be the home of some sort of benevolent spirit that they hadn't wanted loosed, so they had placed arrows all around to signify that their weapons were drawn against it, and that it must stay in the hole to avoid trouble with them. Though the years had rotted away the arrows and left only the points, Gabriel was still extremely serious as he explained this to me. So to humor him I left the arrowheads where they had been placed.

I know now, though it was not evident to me at the time, that the Hurryups were doing all they could to help JudyAnn and me keep our minds off the tragedy our family had experienced. It helped tremendously that neither of them seemed to have any desire to discuss it. Naturally JudyAnn and I talked about our parents at night when we were alone in the lean-to, but we weren't ready to discuss such things with others. Our memories were too precious, too fragile, and neither of us felt like sharing.

Of course, neither of us knew exactly what had happened back in town, either. We were certain that Mother was dead, and we assumed the same for Father, though we didn't actually know. So at night when we were alone we talked about it, imagining the worst, trying to remember each of our parents, and constructing in our memories the features and events we wanted to cling to for the remainder of our lives. JudyAnn cried a lot during those hours, and I admit that I also wept a little. Mainly, though, besides my anger at Carlos, I remember being filled with a dull, aching sense of loneliness that I could not make go away.

I learned more of Gabriel Hurryup's past during the second day out traipsing together. We had walked down a rabbit, which he had then killed with a stone and was roasting over a tiny bit of fire that I hadn't thought would cook anything. Carefully the old man was turning the little spit he had put together out of brush, and slowly the pinkish rabbit meat was beginning to turn brown.

"Wagh!" Gabriel breathed as he finally stopped the spit and pinched a bit of meat from the roasted rabbit, "she smells good as pine hog and better'n painter meat, don't ye think?"

"Pine hog?"

"Aye, lad. Porcupine, with the quills burnt off and the meat roasted pink as rattlesnake flesh." Popping the bit of roasted rabbit in his mouth, he chewed it for a moment, pronounced it "fit for man or beast," and tore off a whole back leg, which he handed to me.

"Shoe leather!" I grimaced after taking a bite and giving it one or two chews. "This tastes awful!"

Gabriel Hurryup cackled with glee. "It be the salt ye be missing, laddie. Me sweet Miss Kizzy has been using it since ye came. But when we be alone, we eat our vittles the way the Injuns do, with no salt nor flavoring, other than smoke and ashes, to foul up the taste."

"I . . . I don't think I can eat it."

"That be your choice, all right." Tearing off the other back leg, the old man took a bite from it and began to chew. "Howsomever, lad," he said between bites, "there won't be nothing more before dark, so me question be, how hungry, exactly, be ye?"

The rumblings inside getting worse, I held my breath, took another bite, and began to chew. And after a few more bites, I almost stopped noticing how much like cardboard the saltless rabbit tasted.

After a few minutes, old Gabriel launched into his storytelling, not paying my grimaces even the least little bit of attention. "It were in eighteen hundred and ought two, lad, that this child became a free trapper. That means I weren't aligned with any of the large fur-trading companies of the time.

"With me pardners Joseph Dickson, Otis Splunkman, and James Kipp, the last of which had once served under the authority of the Columbia Fur Company and so knowed what he were about, this child made a pile of winter trips up the Lower Missouri and, later on, above the yellow waters of the Osage and on to the Upper Missouri.

"On these perilous journeys, which took us from the safety of our homes for a year or more ever time, me pardners and me cut timber, trapped and took beaver plews by the boatload, and had hard doings as mountain men. Aye, we were curly old he-wolves from the high-up hills, fit for fighting man or varmint, and nachural inclined to do both!"

"When," I asked, passing the time, "did you decide to live here on the Dome?"

"Well, laddie," he responded amiably, "that were a strange one, she were. The short of it be that an old Injun brung me here, it were in the spring of the year eighteen and thirty as I recollect, and later on this child decided it were a fine place to plant a home."

"But why?" I asked. "Why would you and Miss Kizzy ever want to live in an awful place like this?"

Gabriel grinned, his mouth full of rabbit meat. "'Tis another story ye be wanting, is it? Well, laddie, I'll oblige ye. But remember that I be telling ye the gospel truth so help me God, and it were well if ye'd be believing."

I said nothing because I no longer had the least notion of how to combat his awful lies, and I suppose he took that as a good sign.

"As I said, it were the spring of the year eighteen and thirty, mid-April, I do believe, and this child were in some hills about four day west of here, figuring to wrap up the season's trapping on the creek I were following. I'd set some traps in one beaver pond and were headed for another, upstream, when in the willows before me I seed an Injun warrior what had been killed—or so it looked—by a monstrous grizz. He were head to toe with blood and gore, a terrible sight, and of a sudden this ol' hoss were holding Betsy to the ready and looking for the grizz what had kilt him. Then that Injun give out with a groan, and I knew I were in near as bad a fix as him.

"Nachural I were of two minds regarding what to do, but after a spell and seeing no sign of the grizz, I lay aside ol' Betsy and turned in to help. Dragging the Injun to the creek I washed him good and proper, and then I daubed him all over with mud and some bear grease of my own, and somewheres along in there he opened his eyes and commenced to studying on me, not skeered nor even worried. But when I tried giving him a drink, he weren't having none of it. Nachural I kept after him, and finally he signaled that he would take a pull from his own water-skin and no other. He done it, and afterward this child took a pull meownself, thinking he had got him some firewater from some company trader somewheres. I spit it out quick, though, on account of it were the most foul-tasting alkali water this son'd ever et!"

"So, it wasn't firewater?"

"Not hardly! By next morning the Injun were doing wondrous, though he hadn't said a word the whole and entire time. I'd tried a little Comanche and Kiowa on him during the night, for we were near to both their countries, but he hadn't answered back. With morning I also tried a little signing, and that were when he finally opened his mouth and showed me his tongue, which had long since been sliced off clean!"

"Sliced off?" I asked, astounded.

"Aye, lad, with a knife. So's he'd know this ol' hoss understood, I showed him me own missing topknot, and his eyes got mighty big and round. Then he started waving his hands fast and furious, talking sign faster'n better than I had ever seed it talked, and the best this child could interpret was that he had been waiting more'n twict as long as a coon's age for me to show up. Yessiree, I were the one the Great Spirit had finally sent to claim some wondrous treasure he knew the secret of, and that I were to follow him to it.

"Nachural," he cackled gleefully, "upon seeing the sign for treasure, I agreed!"

Gabriel went on, explaining that he and the warrior had traveled eastward for four days, and at the beginning and ending of each day the old Indian had performed certain rituals, cleansing both himself and Gabriel so they would be worthy to approach the treasure together. Finally they had arrived at a hillside in some of the most desolate, barren country Gabriel had ever seen. There, after more preparations, the Indian had removed some brush and rocks and revealed a hidden cave into which he had crawled, a bewildered Gabriel following.

"A cave?" I groaned from behind him, thinking of Keziah Jane's imaginary rock cavities that ran all the way to China. "There aren't any caves in this country!"

"And how would ye know that, laddie? Have ye explored it all?"

"No," I admitted grumpily. "I've just never heard of any."

Gabriel Hurryup cackled. "Lad, there be many things in this world ye've never yet heard of. But know ye this, though it were small, that old Injun had led me into a cave, certain! I crawled into the hole after the man, he struck a flint to a torch that was setting handy, and it were then I could see the cave all about me.

"Wagh, lad," Gabriel continued, knowing he had my full attention despite my earnest efforts not to believe what he was saying, "this child don't know what he expected in the way of treasure, leastwise not exact. But what I expected weren't what I found, that were certain. Inside that cave were only two things what might have been out of the ordinary—a small spring of that same terrible-tasting water what the Injun had been packing in his skin and insisting on drinking even when better were available, and the same little seep of oil that be there today."

In the mind of that supposed old Indian these things had been great, great treasures, Gabriel said, guarded by what I assumed was the very spirit he had mentioned earlier—the one held captive by the arrow points. Very powerful, this spirit could either bless or curse in some mysterious manner, and the Indian had done his best to impress that fact upon Gabriel. The Indian had also required of him a solemn promise that he would cherish these treasures, use them only for good, keep the knowledge of them secret, and protect them with his very life. If he would do so, Gabriel had been promised, the spirit who protected them would remain his friend.

It was all the typical ingredients of dime mystery novels, so naturally I was hooked. Still, I couldn't escape the feeling that I'd read it all before. A benevolent spirit guarding treasures! Surely Gabriel Hurryup could come up with something a little more imaginative than that.

"The onliest other thing that ye had maybe ought to know so's your question will be answered," the old trapper then told me, "were that when we were about to leave the cave, that fool Injun pulled out his toe-stabber, threw me onto me back there in the rocks and sand of the cave, grabbed me by the throat, and made to cut out me tongue."

"He *what?*"

"Ye heard me, lad! And being as how this child'd already lost enough of hisself to them red sons to suit both heaven and earth, I fought back. 'Course I knowed he were only trying to protect his big secret the way it had been protected with him, but I hadn't no intention of telling anybody nohow. Besides, when I were to home of a summer I sort of enjoyed palaverin' with me sweet Miss Kizzy and the younguns, and not having a tongue would've made sech palaverin' a tesh harder." Again he cackled at his own strange humor.

"Somewheres in the midst of our little battle, though, the Injun gasped and his eyes went all wide and round and he grabbed at his chest. Then he keeled over sudden and went under! Just like that, he were dead. I reckon his old ticker had stopped plumb cold, for certain it is that this child had not harmed him. So I propped his mortal shell up aside his precious treasures, filled his and me own water skins with enough of that terrible-tasting liquid to carry me through, and plugged the hole to the cave. Then I got meself out of that country fast as I could go, certain I would never return.

"But I tell ye, laddie, a man never knows. There were something about it what kept nagging at me, haunting me, making me wonder about the spirit what that Injun figured had picked me out of all humankind and sent me to him. Nachural I spoke of it to Miss Kizzy, and she began to thinking on it too."

By now the rabbit meat was gone, the sun was sloping toward the west, and the tiny fire was nothing more than fine, white ashes.

"Thirty year later," old Gabriel went on, seemingly oblivious to the passing of time, "both of us still wondering but tired plumb to death of the wandering life and feeling old and wore down, Miss Kizzy and me come back to this God-forsaken country. Why, says ye? Because, says I, this ol' hoss were finally starting to figure out what sort of treasure that sorry old Injun had actual left me."

"It was the oil, wasn't it." I'd made a statement, not asked a question, and Gabriel Hurryup did not respond. Instead he simply threw back his head and cackled, long and loud.

"By then you figured you knew the value of the oil," I stated with disgust when he had finished his laughter, knowing now that he was no different from the people in town who had murdered my parents. "But you were fooled the same as Carlos has fooled us. You thought that oil would make you rich, and instead of making you rich, all it's ever done is help to keep you warm."

"Well, laddie," Gabriel Hurryup replied as he rose and swept his moccasin toward the fire, kicking dirt over the coals, "ye be a thinker, ye be, though for a fact ye were nowise gifted with a nose for the trail. But hearken ye to this, and remember: the warmth from the oil, plus that terrible-tasting water to quench our thirst and revitalize us, be more'n enough to keep Miss Kizzy and me happy for the rest of our days! More, laddie—and this ye can believe or not, as ye wish—from the day we laid the first foundation stone to the home place, it always were."

PART THREE

17

~ It was barely daylight of our third day with the Hurryups when I was awakened by the tinkling and clanking of harness chains and the squeaks and banging of a wagon. It sounded to be directly outside the small window of the lean-to, but somewhere in the midst of getting up to see who it might be, I dropped back off to sleep. A little later I began having a dream about my father and mother talking quietly in their room, just as they had done since before I could remember. The dream seemed to go on and on, Father doing most of the talking, and suddenly my eyes popped open and I knew it was no dream. Father was there! He was outside our lean-to door, speaking quietly, telling someone a long, involved story.

"JudyAnn," I whispered frantically as I pulled on my shirt and struggled into my trousers, "Pop's here! Come on, Jude! Wake up! Father's come for us!"

"Father?" she asked groggily as she sat up in bed, one of Keziah Jane Hurryup's frequently patched, funny old flannel nightgowns twisted all around her. "He's here?"

"Yeah, out there in the big room. Listen. You can hear him talking."

JudyAnn grew still, and in a moment Father's voice came again through the thick wooden door.

"Shhh," I whispered as she gave out a little squeal and jumped to the floor. "Let's surprise him!"

Carefully we opened the door, and there were the Hurryups and a whiskered man I didn't know, all listening intently to Father, who was sitting in Gabriel's chair with his back to us.

Quietly we crept forward, the others giving no sign to warn him that we were behind him, and then did the three of us have a grand reunion! And I don't mind saying that even though I was coming on twelve and maybe should have been more grown up, when Father's arms pulled me close and I could feel his kisses on my head and cheeks, well, I burst out bawling like a baby. JudyAnn did the same, and when I finally looked up again the

Hurryups and that other fellow were gone, leaving the three of us alone in the big room together.

Father was in rough shape, though I hadn't really noticed it at first. His head and chest were wrapped tightly, both his legs were in splints, and one hand and wrist were completely hidden under a mound of white wrappings. One of his eyes was black and blue, and there were other bruises on his face and neck. But his smile was the same, and so was his voice, and he was shedding as many tears as we were.

"Clue and Sis," he said, trying to talk and hug and kiss us all at once, "I am so pleased that you are here! Thank you, Clue, for taking care of your sister in such a courageous way!"

"I was just being obedient," I mumbled, secretly pleased.

Father nodded. "I know, and I can't tell you how proud of you I am!"

"But where have you been?" JudyAnn asked as she studied Father and his extensive white wrappings. "Clue and I have been here with Miss Kizzy and Gabriel forever! And why are you so wrapped up, Father? Did those awful people hurt you like they hurt poor Mother?"

"You mean that lynch-mob who used to be our

friends?" I added bitterly, before Father could reply. "They lynched Mother sure enough, Jude, so why be surprised that they did this to Father? I—Pop, what about Mother? Where is she? I . . . I mean, where—"

Father's tearful eyes instantly betrayed his sorrow and grief, and once again he reached out and pulled us to him. "She passed away yesterday morning, Clue."

"Yesterday? But I thought—"

Reaching up, Father put his finger on my lips, bringing instant silence. "Listen to me, both of you, and I'll try to explain all that has happened. After you and JudyAnn got away, Garner and Vicky Purseman carried your mother into the livery stable and did what they could for her. Meanwhile Ernesto Ribaldo went after Doc Bones—"

"She truly was alive?" I questioned in astonishment.

Father nodded as his eyes dripped silent tears that coursed down his cheeks. "Yes, and conscious, too. She spoke to Vicky Purseman about the two of you—about how much she loved you and wanted to be with you to watch you grow into fine, strong adults. She told Vicky how proud she was of both of you—"

"I didn't make her very proud, Pop! You know how I was always forcing her to harp on me!"

Reaching up, Father gently rubbed my hair. "I know, Clue, and I know how it troubled you. But your mother was fighting something that none of us understood, so if you'll allow me to finish—"

Silently I nodded.

"By the time Doc Bones reached the livery, Abby was unconscious. After wrapping her head as well as he could and giving Ernesto careful instructions, he got the freighter and his wife to take her to the city in one of their light wagons. Ruined all four horses, he ran them so hard, but Ernesto got her to the hospital before the next morning, which as you know is a mighty fast trip. By then she was convulsing something fierce, so the doctors thought she must have slivers of bone imbedded in her brain. Instead they found a large growth—a tumor, they called it—that had apparently been ready to rupture or blow apart for some time. It was just inside her left temple area, and had been creating a lot of pressure and pain."

"Mother's headaches?" I questioned, feeling stunned.

"That's right, Clue, her headaches and irritability, her unclear thinking. The tumor was affecting her in many ways. She had known something was wrong, too. We had even talked about it from time to time. Now we understand what it was." Tenderly Father smiled up at me.

I nodded soberly. This was amazing news, certainly more than I could grasp in those few moments of conversation. In the years since, as I have thought it through, I can see that Father's news did away with most of my anger and guilt. It hadn't been Mother's fault; it hadn't even been mine! We had both been dealt poor hands by an unknown tumor, and so our losses could be laid to it instead of each other. Besides, hadn't she told Vicky Purseman how much she loved me, and how proud of me she was?

But now she was dead! I thought with renewed bitterness as I watched Father's grief. Killed by Carlos and those miserable townspeople—

"The blow from that stone apparently ruptured her tumor," Father was saying, "and that is what took her life. But remember, children. Abby's tumor has been giving her trouble for more than a year now, getting bigger and bigger, and the doctors say it was close to rupturing on its own. Apparently it was a miracle that she lived as long as she did."

"Are . . . are you saying she wasn't murdered?"

Sadly Father shook his head. "Not at all, Clue. Carlos and his lynch-mob killed her sure enough, and they'll bear the burden of it throughout their lives. But instead of us being bitter toward them, which won't do anybody any good, I want the three of us to remember that Abby couldn't have lived much longer anyway. While it's right to miss her and feel lonely for her presence and her love, I think we should try to be thankful that she was taken so quickly, and didn't have to suffer like she most certainly would have."

"But what about Carlos? Or the murderers?" I was trying to push Mother's final words from my mind. "They have to be punished!"

"They will be, Clue, in one way or another. That's the law of justice, and it cannot fail! I'm not yet terribly old, but I've lived long enough to figure out that, in this life, nobody gets away with anything. Oh, it may look like it for a time, I grant you that. But sooner or later justice will be done. We do good things and, sure as shooting, good things will one day come back to us. We do bad things—like Carlos and those other sorry people who killed Abby and tried to kill me—and one day it will all come back to haunt us. You mark my words, both of you. If the law ignores them, and it may, those who killed your mother will end up miserable nonetheless. They will never again feel the peace and happiness they once enjoyed, for happiness cannot be found in wickedness. Not ever!"

"Were you with Mother?" JudyAnn asked, apparently indifferent to Father's profound philosophy.

"No, Sis," Father responded as he turned to JudyAnn, "I wasn't with her. I was hit with a lot of rocks too, and the stoning didn't stop until Garner Purseman came running up with a barrel stave and started beating people off."

"But I thought he was with Mother—"

"He was, Clue. But as soon as he saw her safely on her way with the Ribaldos, he came to my aid—him, John Olson, and Spots Heyermier. They're the three who dispersed the crowd and saved my life."

"One-armed John, Skipper's father?"

"That's right." Father smiled. "Having only one arm didn't slow him down any that I could see. He's a powerful fellow, and a good man to have for a friend."

"But . . . where have you been since then?"

Father's grin increased dramatically. "Hiding out in So-Help-Me Hannah's storm cellar. Between Doc Bones and her, I've had pretty good care, too. Finally last night Otis came for me—"

"Otis?" I asked, trying to keep his story straight in my benumbed mind. "I keep hearing about this Otis, but I have no idea who he is."

"He's Otis Splunkman, Clue—Gabriel's friend, who lives a few miles southwest of here. He was the bearded fellow who was here with us when you came in. When you and JudyAnn showed up a few days ago, Gabriel sent up a smoke signal—"

"A smoke signal?" This seemed to be getting stranger by the minute.

"That's right, son. Apparently Gabriel and Otis learned the art from the Sioux, and for years they have used smoke to keep in touch with each other. So when you two appeared with word of your mother's passing, Gabriel sent up a signal asking Otis for help. Otis tells me he followed your mother to the city and stayed right near her until she was gone. Then he paid for her burial, returned on a hard lope, got his wagon and team of mules, reported in to Gabriel, and came into town for me. Other than catnaps, I don't suppose he has slept a wink in the last four days."

My head was spinning, I was hearing so many new things. The Pursemans, the Ribaldos, One-armed John Olson, Spots Heyermier, So-Help-Me Hannah Tewksberry, Doc Bones, Otis Splunkman—

and Gabriel and Kizzy Hurryup, too? They had all known at least a little of what was going on, and they had all done what they could to help—

"Are we going home now?" JudyAnn asked hopefully. "I miss my dollies—and my own bed."

Again Father's expression betrayed his sadness. "We don't have a home any longer, Sis. Somebody burned it to the ground that first night. Folks say the fire spread to the house after the automobile was set ablaze."

"What?" I practically shouted. "Our new Packard? But I thought—"

"In spite of the fact that we have some wonderful friends, Clue, there are people in town who don't much like me. A lot of them, it turns out."

"But . . . how dare they, after all you've done for them—"

Father smiled sadly. "'I leave behind no enemies save those I have tried to help.' I've heard that Napoleon Bonaparte said that after he was betrayed and on his way into exile. I think I know what he meant."

"I wish I did!" I snarled bitterly.

"One day you will. Despite all the silly things I've been accused of, it all comes down to this: A great many people think I'm standing between them and their families and a whole lot of money—wealth that by right belongs to them. And in a sense, I am. Trouble is, that's a mighty dangerous place to stand, no matter whom you are facing."

"But . . . but there isn't any oil, at least not enough to amount to anything! Gabriel showed me the dry wells."

Father nodded. "I know. He told me the whole story years ago. Sadly, people are going to believe what they want, no matter how much evidence exists to the contrary. Worse, those folks in town aren't through. For days and days now Carlos de Ortega has been filling their heads with mush, and I feel certain they won't rest until this Dome country is theirs."

Suddenly Gabriel and Miss Kizzy were back in the room, their faces somber. Less than a heartbeat later, Otis Splunkman made his appearance.

"Zeke," Gabriel said as he placed a hand on Father's shoulder, "Otis says the mob be coming from town, a whole raft of 'em, and be nearly here to the home place. It be time, I be thinking, to finally make a stand!"

18

"The lynch-mob's here again?" I asked, my heart suddenly in my throat.

"Aye, lad." Gabriel Hurryup laid his hand on my shoulder. "And I hope them sons've been enjoying the weather, because, says I, where me sweet Miss Kizzy and me be fixing to send 'em, they'll be turning hot in a hurry!" For a moment old Gabriel gave out with his joy-filled cackle. "Zeke," he said then, abruptly serious, "have ye the papers I gave ye?"

Silently Father tapped the breast of his tattered tweed coat.

"What papers?" I blurted, astounded that none of them seemed overly concerned about us facing another crazed mob.

"Gabriel's deed to the Dome, Clue, plus a couple of other things. Garner Purseman got them out of the bank so I could have them re-recorded in the city. Now, no more questions. We need to do some fast thinking—"

"Aye, and acting," Gabriel growled as he quickly turned open the large valves next to his stoves and fireplace. "Otis, betwixt us I reckon we can carry Zeke here into the cave. Me sweet Miss Kizzy'll bring the younguns."

"But why—" I started to argue. I say *started*, because Father didn't let me get very far at all.

"Cluvarous," he said, gritting his teeth against the pain as he was being lifted out of the chair, "*not now!*"

Closing my mouth in surprise, I followed JudyAnn and Keziah Jane through one of the two rear doors I had never seen opened, on through a sort of curved tunnel, and finally out into cool, pitch-black darkness. Quickly, however, a lantern was lit. My mind in a whirl, I stared about me while JudyAnn whispered something to Mrs. Hurryup and Father submitted to being lowered onto a low couch.

It was a cave we were standing in! One of Miss Kizzy's cavities in the rock! In that country of no caves that I had ever heard of, we were in what seemed to me a large cave, obviously the one Gabriel Hurryup had told me about the day before.

Somewhere I could hear water running, and in the glow from the lantern I was even able to see a low, curved wall of mortared stone, and behind it a pool of shiny blackness. To my astonishment I could also see, propped beside the low wall, the ghastly, whitened bones of a human skeleton.

"Otis, be ye staying here with the Joneses? It be the thing Miss Kizzy and me would ask of ye."

Silently Otis Splunkman nodded his willingness.

"Good." Gabriel Hurryup smiled down at JudyAnn and me. "Now, me bonnie laddie and sweet wee lassie, it were a pleasure, certain sure! Ye be fine folk, and brave, and me and me sweet Miss Kizzy be honored with the knowing of ye. Had they lived, we'd have liked our own younguns to be like the two of ye, exact. Now don't ye be skeered, not for a moment. The spirit that old Injun told me about be still here, still protecting the place. More, I've rigged up these doings a bit meownself, to give the spirit a hand, so to speak. So ye'll be safe as a summer's day!"

Quickly Gabriel took Keziah Jane by the arm, and together they started back through the tunnel.

"But . . . but wait!" I shouted, my voice echoing in the cave and sounding unnaturally high and squeaky, even for me. "Where're you going?"

Instantly Gabriel Hurryup turned his piercing blue eyes back upon me. "Laddie, the side of the rooster what grows the most feathers for plucking is always the outside!" Briefly he cackled, then grew instantly serious again. "Me 'n me sweet Miss Kizzy have been layin' about the home place a bit too long, says I, and be hankerin' for another trek. It be time."

"But . . . the mob!" I pleaded, trying meanwhile to decipher the meaning behind roosters and feathers, for I had finally figured out that Gabriel Hurryup's strange stories usually had a point to them. "It's coming from town!"

"Aye, that be so."

"They . . . they'll see you! They—"

"Ahhh, me fine laddie," Gabriel Hurryup then declared, his voice growing low and fierce, "I be speaking truth pure and simple when I say that they don't know who they be dealing with. Just ye remember, Cluvarious Jones, I be a mountain man, sure and true! I be a trapper and a trader and a curly old he-wolf from the high-up hills, and me sweet Miss Kizzy be meaner'n me! Wagh!"

Abruptly Gabriel Hurryup broke into his wild, joyful cackle, his eyes flashing and his body doubling over, and I finally realized that the old mountain man was actually looking forward to what was coming—the plucking of the feathers on the outside of his rooster.

"Me Gabe darlin' be right, laddie," Keziah Jane agreed, sounding much more calm than her husband. "They've opened the ball, them foolish souls out yonder, and now it be time for every man-jack one of them to dance! What them sorry folks don't know, but be about to discover, is that it'll be me and me Gabe darlin' what'll be calling the tune!"

Keziah Jane then smiled as brightly as old Gabriel, and after she had given both JudyAnn and me a sly wink, clucked "Doo-da dah" a few more times, and instructed us not to worry, she turned and followed her husband back through the tunnel, closing the door behind her.

19

"Pop? Pop, what's happening?"

With the rest of us, Father was staring into the dark and empty tunnel where the Hurryups had gone. "I don't know, Clue," he responded quietly. "Gabriel wouldn't tell me anything except that he had a bit of a surprise prepared if the mob should happen to come. But remember, son, he told us not to worry."

"I'm not worried, Father." JudyAnn had forced a wide smile onto her face.

"That's my sweetheart," Father purred as he gathered her to him on the couch. "Here, Father will hold you tight—"

Dizzy with fear for the Hurryups as well as for ourselves, I began turning about, probing with my eyes into the darkness of the cave, trying desperately to think of what I could do—what any of us could do. We were all in danger, I knew it, and there had to be some way—

Realizing that my foot was stumbling over something, I looked down and was not in the least surprised to see, glinting in the lantern light, the long metal blade of an old-fashioned knife. The Indian's toe-stabber, I thought as I bent down and picked it up—the very one meant to slice off Gabriel's tongue. *Wagh, indeed!* I thought with amazement. All along old Gabriel Hurryup had been telling me the gospel truth, even about that old Indian who had died of a heart attack in the midst of their fight.

Strange that the blade was made of metal, though. Somehow I'd pictured it to be chipped stone, like the arrowheads that ringed the hole up on top of the hill—

Instantly my mind seized upon that hole, and in the same instant I knew perfectly well that it was an escape route from this terrible cave. By then the silent Otis Splunkman had lit another lantern and a couple of oil-soaked torches, and these were giving off a fair amount of smoke.

Taking up one of the torches, and remembering a plot out of one of my infamous dime novels, I watched which way the smoke was drifting. Slowly I walked in that direction, which was farther back into the cave, reassuring Father as I went that I would stay out of mischief. Soon I had turned a slight bend and found the pool of water from which Gabriel and Keziah Jane Hurryup had piped their culinary supply. It had been carefully walled, just as the oil seep had been, and I could see from Gabriel's hollow pipe how this well had also been tapped for the Hurryups' use. But by then the cave floor had begun sloping upward, a dim light showed ahead, and so I moved on.

For another thirty yards I climbed freely, and then the cave narrowed dramatically and began twisting sharply upward. It was from up there, I could now see, that the light was showing.

Propping the torch with some rocks and thrusting the old knife under my belt, I scrambled upward, and was soon thankful that I had not yet reached my growth. The cave was now nothing more than a hole twisting up through the earth, tight and confining. But I had little difficulty pulling myself through it, and soon was rewarded with sunlight so bright I had to squint my eyes. Without thought I slid across the ring of arrowheads, pushing them aside in my haste. Scrambling to my feet, I took out the old Indian's knife to hold it away from my body, and at a dead run started for where the hill dropped steeply off to the cabin.

I don't know what made me stop before I got to the edge—maybe a sixth sense or something. But stop I did, and it was while I was bent over with my hands on my knees, catching my breath, that I heard the terrifying rumble of angry voices.

Thinking of how Gabriel had once described going against his Rickaree enemies, I dropped to my belly and squirmed forward, the knife still in my hand. In that way I came carefully to the edge of the hill, screened from below by a small bush I had intentionally kept between me and whoever might have been looking upward. And even though I thought I knew what to expect, I was completely unprepared for what I saw.

Below me, ringing the front and sides of the Hurryup cabin but back some little distance, were what I guessed to be upwards of a hundred people. I say people because there may have been women there as well as men. I couldn't tell, for all of them had their faces painted black and were dressed as men, and the way they were shrieking and carrying on, it was impossible to tell their gender. Neither could I recognize any but one of them, though I had no doubt I would have known them all if I could have somehow removed their evil-looking black paint.

The one I recognized? It was friend Carlos, painted like the others but his voice and fluttering hands so obvious, even from the ridge-top, that I knew him in an instant.

It was sobering to lie there listening to the parents of at least some of my friends, as well as a goodly number of our family's neighbors, associates, and fellow church members, jeering and yelling their horrid, pathetic taunts and insults at the unseen Hurryups.

In the center of the mob, looking more cold and deadly than it had ever seemed, was our town's famed Civil War cannon, the same one old Doc Bones had fired off every Fourth of July for as long as anyone could remember. Somehow those black-hearted souls had hauled that terrible weapon all the way from town, and it was down there now, squared off in front of the Hurryup cabin and pointed right at it, ready to do their bidding.

It wasn't Doc Bones preparing to fire, I knew, for he was Father's friend and wouldn't put up with such nonsense. But some black-faced mobber was definitely behind that cannon holding a torch, and others with rifles stood menacingly around him.

"All right, people," one of the mobbers who stood near Carlos shouted, "listen up! Do you hear me? *Listen up!*"

There was a stirring and a gradual quieting of the dark-faced assemblage.

"You all know why we're here! Carlos has been good enough to change his mind and give us until today to clear this Dome so he can do his drilling. Otherwise he's gone, and so is the money we might have had from all the oil he's discovered here."

"Are those crazy Indians even in there?"

"I imagine. But if they aren't and their home is nothing but rubble when they return, you can bet they'll be gone again in a hurry."

"Just like their crazy name—"

"Yeah!" several shouted.

"All right, so none of us will feel more responsible than the others, we'll do this like the state does its executions! We'll all count down together in unison, starting at ten, to fire the cannon. After the four cannon balls we brought with us have leveled the place, and if they're needed, we'll all throw our torches onto the rubble and then get out of here. Any questions?"

"Aye, lads, this ol' hoss has a question, certain sure!"

I was so surprised by Gabriel Hurryup's piercing

voice that I nearly jumped to my feet. I didn't, but I certainly strained myself trying to see him. Because I couldn't, I have been forced to assume that he was still in the cabin, yelling out of one of the small windows.

"Who's that?" The leader's voice sounded strained, surprised. *"Who was that?"*

"Why, I be one of the two people ye folks call the Hurryups," Gabriel screeched. "Aye, and the other—me sweet Miss Kizzy, she be called—be standing beside me. We be a couple of far-traveling children from the high-up hills, lads, and now we be fixing to lift some hair. Be ye ready?"

"Now see here, you crazy Indian!" This was Carlos shouting. "You can't just—"

"Friend Carlos, hear ye this for the last and final time, and all of ye remember it! I be no Indian, and neither be me sweet Miss Kizzy. Of a truth, though, this ol' hoss'd rather a hundred times over be a bloody Rickaree with a thousand honest scalps on his lance than a black-faced, lynch-mobbing coward of the likes of ye!"

"I tell you," Carlos shrieked, his hands fluttering in the air, "we will not—"

"That were me question," Gabriel shouted, cutting him off again, "or leastwise a part of it! The

rest of it were: Be ye ready? Be ye ready to spend
the rest of your days sick near to death with the
knowing that for money ye have committed awful
murder, and that in a most foul and cold-blooded
way? Aye, be ye ready to spend the rest of your
nights sweating and dreaming of the same, watching me sweet Miss Kizzy and me a-comin' at ye in
your minds and not sleeping hardly a'tall with the
terror of it? What be your answer, people? Be ye
ready?"

"Listen to us!" another black-faced mobber
yelped, almost as if he were pleading. "We've tried
reason, we've tried—"

"If ye be ready," Gabriel's voice was now shrill
and fierce, cutting the man off in midsentence,
"then let 'er blow, lads! *Let 'er blow!*"

"And doo-da dah to the bunch of ye!" Keziah Jane
Hurryup shouted immediately afterward, her voice
gleeful and yet every bit as fierce as her husband's.

In the shocked silence that followed, a desperate
Carlos shouted, "TEN." Seconds later a few around
him mumbled "NINE," a lot more shouted "EIGHT,"
and the terrible countdown had begun.

I lay mesmerized, the volume of the countdown
rising higher with each descending number. I was
holding my breath in anticipation of the Hurryups

firing their own weapons from within the cabin. But that didn't happen, and just when I remembered that Gabriel's old Betsy rifle didn't have a flint or hold a charge and so couldn't fire, I saw the black-faced man behind the cannon lower his torch and touch the fuse in unison with the overwhelming shout of "FIRE!"

There was a moment's pause, the counting crowd grew silent with anticipation, and then all hell seemed to break loose! A booming, fiery explosion literally lifted me off the earth—an explosion far more severe than a single cannon shot would warrant.

Dust, smoke, and flames were everywhere, more explosions followed, people were screaming in pain and confusion, and then I could see that fire was not only billowing from the cabin's ruins but raining down and burning in a hundred places scattered across the bench.

Oil, I thought with sudden understanding! It was raining burning oil! And it was all those indiscriminately burning fires that were wringing the cries of pain and fear from the panic-stricken mob.

With tears of grief and anger streaming down my face, I gripped the old knife and prepared to fly down the hill and destroy Carlos and every other coward who had just blown the Hurryup cabin to bits—yes, and my new friends the Hurryups with it! No longer was I afraid of those black-faced people, for suddenly my mind was filled with Mother's account of the huge tomatoes, and I knew as certainly as she had that the mob had no additional weapon that could make me flinch! Yes, sir, it was time for Cluvarous Jones to take revenge—

Just as I was gathering strength to launch myself down the hill, however, an arm settled across my shoulders and I remained pinned to the earth. "Wagh, hoss," a voice breathed softly from beside me, "ol' Gabriel were always a good'un for startin' things off with a bang, he were."

Twisting in surprise, I was dumbfounded to see Otis Splunkman lying on his belly beside me with his arm holding me down, a look of immense satisfaction on his bearded face. How he had come to be there I couldn't guess, nor how long he had lain beside me. All I knew was that he was there, had saved me from what was likely certain death, and had witnessed the same terrible things I had seen.

"Were . . . were the Hurryups in the ca . . . cabin?" My heart felt like it was breaking, and I was crying far harder than I had ever cried over my mother's death. Or maybe, now that I think of it, hers was the death I was really crying over. I don't know. I just felt like my whole world was filled with pain, and that no matter how good the people were that I loved and cared about, somebody was going to come along and kill them! "Did . . . you see them get out before that . . . that cannonball exploded?"

For a long moment the bearded man ignored me. "Aye, boy," he finally breathed, his eyes never leaving the scattered, already beaten mob, "he were a fighter, Gabriel were. Fought the hardest and the smartest of any man I ever seed. The onliest one to ever get off scot-free were that Rickaree what took his topknot, and Gabriel learned a powerful lot from that mistake, a powerful lot indeed.

"Now, boy, ye've seed it, too!"

Sliding backward, Otis grabbed my boot and pulled me after him. "Your father and sister be worried," was the only other thing he said, and then my old knife was in his free hand and his other arm was around me, holding me up while I continued to sob out my grief and loneliness in a rushing torrent that I thought would never end.

⚬ 20

   Except for a few minor details, there is little left to tell. From Spots Heyermier's newspaper accounts, I learned that within a day or so after the explosion, Carlos de Ortega had signed up practically every adult in town to receive a tiny share of royalties from his newly discovered ocean of oil.

Within a month the Dome was swarming with company men and equipment. Wells were drilled for miles around in every spot that looked somewhat promising, and the twelve-mile stretch of road from the Dome to town was crowded day and night with soon-to-be millionaires, the townsfolk who couldn't keep away.

The one place they wouldn't go near, drillers or townsfolk alike, was the ruins of the Hurryup cabin. Without doubt, Gabriel and Keziah Jane Hurryup had perished in the explosion and fire that had destroyed their home, and that fact alone may have deterred folks from searching there. But Skip Olson once told me that beginning almost immediately after the fire, various people reported seeing the Hurryups—or their ghosts—fast-walking through and around the old place in the dark of night.

The funny thing is, after the explosion Otis and I did quite a bit of quick-stride prowling around at night ourselves, poking through the ruins and just keeping an eye on things. We never found the remains of the Hurryups, for the fire had been too intense to leave that sort of thing behind. But we did find a hidden opening in the cabin floor with steps that dropped down into Miss Kizzy's rock cavity or cistern, the impossibly deep cavern that she had thought might run all the way to China.

Nevertheless, in all my nightly gallivanting with Otis I never once saw the ghosts of the Hurryups, and I never much thought of myself as a ghost or a haunt, either. Still, it had to have been Otis and me those folks had reported seeing, for we were the only ones around. I guess there's no telling what guilt will do to a frenzied mind.

Father, JudyAnn, Otis, and I ended up staying in the cave for the next three weeks while Father's body healed, living off the food supplies the Hurryups had stored there, drinking their funny-tasting water, and just plain taking it easy.

Late one night, after Otis and I had enlarged our hole, and just before I encircled it again with the old arrowheads, we pulled Father and JudyAnn through. Then Otis delivered us to the city in his wagon—a two-day pull. There Father took care of Gabriel's deed and other papers, he and Otis swore out legal depositions concerning all that had happened, and we put a proper marker on Mother's grave. Afterward the three of us boarded the train and headed east.

Otis Splunkman used to think that Gabriel Hurryup had purposely rigged the big explosion that had destroyed his home, either to disperse the mob or, better yet, to teach them a lesson they would never forget. It was a tantalizing thought, filled with glory. But Gabriel could not possibly have known that the lynch-mob would be bringing a cannon with them. And of course it was the exploding cannonball that had ignited the huge firestorm.

No one knows for sure, but I give it as my opinion that Gabriel had certainly made some preparations. He had rigged the tunnel between his home and the cave with some sort of small explosive device so it would collapse when fired, thus sealing off the cave. Certainly that is what Otis and I found had happened when we crawled back down into the cave that day in 1904. The roof directly above the tunnel had collapsed, and the cave had sealed tight, shutting in both the water and the oil. After all, those were the dead Indian's treasures that old Gabriel was sworn to protect.

He may also have planned for fire to destroy his home. I had seen him intentionally open all the valves to his well of oil, allowing it to flood the house. He would have done that for no other reason.

What he couldn't have counted on, I believe, was the cannonball and a small natural-gas vent in some rocks just outside the cabin—a vent that I didn't discover until years later. That natural gas, and the mob's exploding cannonball, set things off in a way no one could have predicted. No doubt the ensuing inferno caught Gabriel and Keziah Jane Hurryup as unawares as it did the mob, only with more disastrous results.

That some of the townsfolk got burned was simply a consequence of their own actions, and not a part of some malicious scheme that Gabriel and his wife had concocted. Such a scheme seems against their natures.

But whether intended or not, some curious things soon began happening in town. Though nothing was ever done to Carlos or the other parties who had been guilty of so much murder and mayhem, at least so far as the law was concerned, they did begin to pay. According to my friend Skip, folks began waking up of a morning to find one or another of their neighbors gone, moved away in the dark of night with neither forwarding address nor fond farewells. By the time the big eastern company's unsuccessful drillers had packed up and gone, with not so much as a teaspoon of oil to show for their efforts, our little community had become practically a ghost town, most of the folks remaining being those who had refused to mob or to accept the promise of royalties from Carlos's fictitious ocean of oil.

Skipper's family were among the last to leave, and when they did, they went to the city. There his father ultimately built a fine new roller mill, which Skip took over after his father passed away. And when Skip died, back in 1962, my wife and I were able to attend his funeral.

Somehow I wasn't surprised to learn, while we

were there for the services, that the creek in our snug little valley had long since dried up. The only signs left to indicate that a fine, progressive community had once existed there were some dying fruit trees, several piles of rotting lumber, and a few crumbling foundations. I'd be amazed if even those exist today.

Both JudyAnn and I have spent a great deal of time pondering the life and death of our mother and what it wrought. It should go without saying that it was hard and lonely without her, and some aspects of her death caused within us certain difficulties and weaknesses—including varying degrees of bitterness toward those who caused it. Those emotions we have had to address.

I suppose life without Mother was even worse for Father, though I never heard him speak of it in those terms. Occasionally I did find him in tears with her photograph in his hands—one he had sent to his parents that was therefore preserved from the fire. And more than once I heard him talking to her when he thought he was alone, pouring out his loneliness and grief or, and this was more frequent, his hopes and joys. Yet when we spoke of her together, it was always the happy times he reminded us of, the loving times, and the great amount of good she had managed to accomplish in her short life.

Once I remember expressing in front of him some bitterness that her murder had gone unavenged. I will never forget how he took me to JudyAnn's room and sat us down together. He then explained his conviction—and he was adamant about this—that all things worked together for good so long as we were doing our best to do right, and that hard times built more solid strength in a human being than any other kind of experience, so long as they were handled with a positive attitude instead of criticism and bitterness.

"Your mother is now with each of you all the time," he told us then and many times thereafter, "instead of just when you might be at home. That is a great and wonderful thing! I believe she's making certain that you understand correctly the things she did her best to teach you when she was here. If I were in your places, Cluvarous and JudyAnn, I would give some serious thought to what I was showing her in response."

Both JudyAnn and I took that to heart, and from time to time we have each felt her presence and her encouragement.

Like Mother, JudyAnn became an educator who

uses firm discipline sprinkled with a liberal dose of love, and in addition to her own marvelous family, she has influenced for good many hundreds of youngsters who have attended her classes.

But her resemblance to our mother goes deeper than that, much deeper. Yes, she is tall like our mother, with the same dark eyes and olive complexion, the same smile, the same tilted head and wonderful politeness. But what amazes me is that I continue to see in her the same dignified but unconquerable spirit that I witnessed in Mother the day she marched off down that dusty road in defense of Father.

As for myself, to my great surprise I finally obtained my growth and turned out tall like Father. But other than that, my life has been far more ordinary than either his or JudyAnn's. I studied law, got involved in some research, and wrote a few books that would bore most folks to tears. What with doing my best over the years to help where I could, we have all managed to have sufficient for our needs.

Mother's death drew us much closer as a family than we might otherwise have been. With one or two minor exceptions, I don't think there has ever been a week when JudyAnn and I have not spoken with each other. She has always been one of my closest confidants and friends, and I don't recall a single incidence of her ever betraying my trust. I have endeavored to treat her the same, and I love her with all my heart.

Father passed peacefully away in the fall of 1959, Mother's name on his lips. But before he died, he told us a couple of things we had never known. First, the papers Gabriel and Keziah Jane Hurryup had given Father that morning before the explosion were their last will and testament. Father had had them recorded in the city at the same time he had rerecorded the infamous deed to the Dome country.

In the will, a copy of which Father gave us on his deathbed, Otis Splunkman was granted the right to live on the Dome for the remainder of his natural life. Additionally, JudyAnn and I were named as the Hurryups' only living heirs. That meant that for more than half a century, despite our ignorance of the fact, the Dome country had been legally ours.

Of course it was a barren, useless place, and since we had homes and lives of our own to live, worlds away from the Dome, neither of us gave it much thought. Still, there were nights when I would lie awake wondering, much as Gabriel must have done, about the treasure in the cave that had meant so much to him and the old Indian. Yes, and about the powerful spirit who had for so long protected the treasure from marauders. Apparently JudyAnn was wondering the same.

In 1964 we started talking with each other about it, and by 1976 we had returned and built two lovely homes. Using modern machinery, we managed to excavate the cavern that had been sealed off by Gabriel's cunning so many years before. Miraculously, we found his trickle of oil still intact, though the bones of the old Indian were unaccountably gone. We used the oil and natural gas to heat and light our homes, and Gabriel's spring to green up the area and fill our culinary needs. JudyAnn's second husband was excited for the chance to come here to stay, but my wife—my third wife, that is, the first two having gone on to their eternal rewards—put up somewhat of a fuss. But she loves it now, and would think of living nowhere else. Neither would any of the rest of us.

As for the geologist, I have no idea what finally happened to the man his parents had so hopefully named Jose Maria Carlos Louis Rivera Sebastian de Ortega Rejos. From time to time I heard some little thing or other, but after a few years I managed to take my father's advice to heart and put bitter thoughts of him away. And as Mother promised, for most of this century I have been a happy man.

I have not yet mentioned the second thing our father told JudyAnn and me before he passed away. And actually it wasn't much, hardly even worth bringing up. It was simply Gabriel Hurryup's crazy opinion as to why he and his sweet Miss Kizzy had lived so long while still appearing so young. And of course my belief continues—that Gabriel's memory of those long-past years and dates was thoroughly confused. That can happen to an old man, and quite frequently does.

Nowadays it is quiet here on the Dome, or mostly so. Even today there are not many folks around. But, modern transportation being what it is, our children, grandchildren, and now more than a few great- and even great-great grandchildren come and go with ease. Both JudyAnn and I are even thinking of adding a few more bedrooms to our homes, our families are growing so large.

To make my point, at this very moment there are two entire baseball teams of youngsters making a whale of a racket out in the yard. And every one of them—every last one—is a child either of my wife and me or of JudyAnn and her husband. That's what I mean about large families.

I promised them this morning that I would show them how to smack a baseball like the record-setting hitters Mark McGwire and Sammy Sosa. They're getting impatient, and Otis Splunkman has just signaled through the window that JudyAnn has dismissed her class and is now out there with them, waiting—

Yes, I believe he is the same Otis Splunkman I've been speaking of all along. And yes, if it actually is Otis Splunkman out there, he'd have to be well over two hundred years old—an unthinkable age for any human being to reach! And no, he certainly doesn't look to be that old. Of course, after the explosion and fire I didn't see him for nearly ninety years, and I was only eleven when I met him the first time, so I might be mistaken. Logically this fellow must be either the grandson or great-grandson of the Otis Splunkman I knew. Still, he looks the same, and he talks the same, and when he showed up a couple of years ago after having lived abroad for some time, we had some wonderful reminiscences to share. But of course that might mean anything—anything at all!

Those other folks out with the children are the McCaigs, as they call themselves. A youngish-looking couple with bright eyes and berry-brown skin, they came with Otis when he flew in from Scotland. Now they spend their days either playing with our children or traipsing around and about this Dome country of ours, telling our youngsters all sorts of tall tales and keeping every single one of us in stitches.

Of course old Gabriel Hurryup claimed to be Scottish, and I have wondered if this couple might be his descendants—several generations removed, of course. Of a truth, however, I don't know. The Hurryups' old Gaelic Bible, the only thing that might have linked them officially to folks in Scotland, vanished with them in the explosion and fire nearly a hundred years ago. Like the Hurryups' remains, the fire left no trace of it behind.

But that funny-talking couple yonder, who are in such an all-fired hurry whenever they go anywhere at all, do seem to like it here. In fact, from the day of their arrival they seemed to know the place better than I, and acted like they had come home. So who knows? Maybe they have.

That'd suit JudyAnn and me just fine. Besides, they don't eat much, and absolutely the only thing they'll drink, day or night, is regular quaffs of the funny-tasting water that still flows from Gabriel's well.